KU-148-101

Antoine Laurain is the award-winning author of seven previous novels including *The Red Notebook* and *The President's Hat.* His books have been translated into twenty-five languages and sold more than 200,000 copies in English. He lives in Paris.

Louise Rogers Lalaurie is a writer and translator from the French. She is based in France and the UK.

Megan Jones is a translator. She lives in London.

Praise for *Red Is My Heart*:

'Both enchanting and disturbing. A heartbroken lover's obsession with his ex is reflected in both images and words' *Washington Post*

'This inspired combination of romantic musings and playful drawings is a collaboration between two great Parisians' *Daily Mail*

'The emotional journey of a broken heart laid bare by an exceptional writer' Jenny O'Brien, author of *Buried Lies*

Praise for *The Readers' Room*:

'The plot blends mystery with comedy to great effect, and, as ever, Laurain has fun at the expense of his countrymen' *Daily Mail*

'A cracking literary murder mystery' *Tatler*

'Laurain has spun a fantastically intricate web here, where the smallest detail could be significant, and, no matter how sure you are that you've grasped it, he is one step ahead. Joyously far-fetched and metafictional' *The Herald*

'[An] elegantly written little gem… the whole thing is such fun' *The Big Issue*

'A stylish whodunnit blended with an affectionate send-up of the world of books' *Sunday Mirror*

'A brief blackly comic masterpiece… An observation on life's rich tapestry; absurd, witty, truthful and engaging' *Crime Time*

'Clever, intricate and a thoroughly satisfying mystery' William Ryan, bestselling author of *House of Ghosts*

Praise for *Vintage 1954*:

'A glorious time-slip caper… Just wonderful' *Daily Mail*

'Delightfully nostalgic escapism set in a gorgeously conjured Paris of 1954' *Sunday Mirror*

'Like fine wine, Laurain's novels get better with each one he writes... a charming and warm-hearted read' Phaedra Patrick, author of *The Curious Charms of Arthur Pepper*

Praise for *Smoking Kills*:

'Funny, superbly over-the-top... not a page too much' *The Times*

'Formidable – and essential packing for any French summer holiday' *Daily Mail*

'A brisk black comedy... Laurain's considered tale retains an elegant detachment... And it does, fittingly, make cigarettes seem seductive again, even to committed non-smokers' *The Observer*

Praise for *The Portrait*:

'A delightful literary soufflé that fans of his other charming books will savor' *Library Journal*

Praise for *French Rhapsody*:

'Beautifully written, superbly plotted and with a brilliant twist at the end' *Daily Mail*

'The novel has Laurain's signature charm, but with the added edge of greater engagement with contemporary France' *Sunday Times*

Praise for *The Red Notebook*:

'A clever, funny novel... a masterpiece of Parisian perfection'
HM Queen Consort

'In equal parts an offbeat romance, detective story and a clarion call for metropolitans to look after their neighbours... Reading *The Red Notebook* is a little like finding a gem among the bric-a-brac in a local brocante'
The Telegraph

'Resist this novel if you can; it's the very quintessence of French romance' *The Times*

'Soaked in Parisian atmosphere, this lovely, clever, funny novel will have you rushing to the Eurostar post-haste... A gem' *Daily Mail*

'An endearing love story written in beautifully poetic prose. It is an enthralling mystery about chasing the unknown, the nostalgia for what could have been, and most importantly, the persistence of curiosity'
San Francisco Book Review

Praise for *The President's Hat*:

'A hymn to la vie Parisienne… enjoy it for its fabulistic narrative, and the way it teeters pleasantly on the edge of Gallic whimsy' *The Guardian*

'Flawless… a funny, clever, feel-good social satire with the page-turning quality of a great detective novel' Rosie Goldsmith

'A fable of romance and redemption' *The Telegraph*

'Part eccentric romance, part detective story… this book makes perfect holiday reading' *The Lady*

'Its gentle satirical humor reminded me of Jacques Tati's classic films, and, no, you don't have to know French politics to enjoy this novel' *Library Journal*

AN ASTRONOMER IN LOVE

AN ASTRONOMER IN LOVE

Antoine Laurain

Gallic Books
London

A Gallic Book

This book is supported by the Institut français (Royaume-Uni)
as part of the Burgess programme.

First published in France as *Les Caprices d'un astre* by Flammarion, Paris

First published in Great Britain in 2023 by
Gallic Books, 12 Eccleston Street, London, SW1W 9LT

A CIP record for this book is available from the British Library

Typeset in Fournier by Gallic Books

ISBN 978-1-913547-46-2

Printed in the UK by CPI (CR0 4YY)
2 4 6 8 10 9 7 5 3 1

This book is dedicated to Guillaume Le Gentil (1725–1792).
A luckless astronomer, an honest soul, and a true hero.

The sun is the shadow of God
Michelangelo

On the twenty-sixth of March 1760, Guillaume Joseph Hyacinthe Jean-Baptiste Le Gentil de La Galaisière, astronomer to the Académie Royale des Sciences, boarded the fifty-gun ship *Le Berryer* in the French port of Lorient, bound for India. As the naval vessel put to sea, he just about managed to cling to the mast – his silver-buckled, patent-leather shoes had almost caused him to lose his footing on the slippery deck. A stiff Breton gale whipped his blue frock coat and lace jabot, and he pressed his right hand firmly to the crown of his three-cornered black felt hat. The start of a long and perilous voyage. When a man set sail to journey halfway around the globe, there was no knowing, in those days, whether he would be seen alive again. Guillaume Le Gentil was travelling on the orders of His Majesty Louis XV, charged with a precise mission – for which he was most uniquely qualified – to measure, with the aid of his telescopes and astronomical instruments, the true (rather than the supposed) distance from the Earth to the sun, on the occasion of the transit of Venus across our star.

The small planet named for the Goddess of Love took an unusual sequence of turns across the sun's disc, to say the least: one passage was followed by a second 8 years later, after which a whole 122 years would pass before the next. Then another 8 year interval, but after that, it would be 105 years until another transit could be observed.

The alternating sequence of 8, 122 and 105 years was unchanged since the creation of the universe itself.

Guillaume Le Gentil had taken every care not to miss the exceptional observations he would make from Pondicherry on 6 June 1761, more than a year after his departure from France. Thanks to which he might, perhaps, become the first man to measure the true distance between the Earth and the star that is the source of all its light.

Everything was prepared down to the last detail, and yet nothing whatsoever would go as planned.

Breathe.

You are alive.

Everything is fine.

You are sitting down. Feel the weight of your body, the weight of your feet and your hands.

Take note of the sounds that surround you.

The familiar female voice was reassuring. It was the same for every session. Xavier Lemercier was on his fifteenth daily session of so-called 'mindful' meditation. This scientific practice had been one of his discoveries when he'd tried to quit smoking. Until now, Xavier had never got into meditation, and as a matter of principle he was hesitant about this sort of thing, imagining it to be full of obscure phrases, with echoes of the New Age and cheap shamanism. 'Imagine you are a fox. Feel the flower within you.' 'Turn your heart towards the eternal Planet Gaia, nurturing mother of all living things.' But that wasn't the case with the app he had downloaded, the only goal of which was to establish thirty-minute pauses each day, and to quieten the frenetic buzz of thoughts that intruded upon every moment like so many wasps. Now the habit of returning to the voice and its soothing phrases was almost as pleasant as pouring oneself a cold aperitif on a sunny terrace after a day's work. For thirty minutes a day, Xavier almost managed to forget his worries, which, for him, was no small feat.

Now, when you feel ready, leave your thoughts behind and let's begin the body scan.

The body scan consisted of mentally sweeping the body, from the tip of your toes to the top of your head, locating any points of discomfort. Xavier often noted a pain in his lower back and a tightness in his stomach.

He had been anxious for two long months. His estate agency was stagnating. Sales were inexplicably few and far between. Admittedly, the Parisian market was over-inflated; prices weren't going down, but by 2012 fewer people were interested in buying and selling property. The usual indicators – household consumption, buying power, the stock market – hardly accounted for the weak sales. But the 'market stakeholders', according to their sacred slogan, all gave the same report: not much was going on at the moment. The most robust among them were unfazed, or seemed to be, but the more fragile ones were beginning to ask themselves questions. The Lemercier and Bricard agency had been well established for twenty years now. Xavier had started out in the Parisian real-estate market with a friend from business school. Now forty-seven years old, Xavier was left as the sole head of Lemercier and Bricard. When someone asked for 'Monsieur Bricard', Xavier replied, calmly, that he was on a business trip. An agency with two names lent it a more reputable air, suggesting a solid team and numerous colleagues at the ready.

Bruno Bricard, his partner who was 'on a business trip', had suddenly decided to return to the countryside two years ago. Tired of city life, tired of all the commuting and the pollution, he told his friend that he wanted to sell his shares. Along with his wife and two children, he had overhauled his life by buying, for the price of their Parisian apartment, a seventeenth-century mansion with eighteen hectares of land in the Dordogne, which they planned to turn into a bed and breakfast. During his last months at the agency, Bruno had tried over and over again to convince Xavier to do the same, with persuasive drawings, surveys and projections detailing how cities would soon become saturated with fine particulate matter and pollution, invaded by cars that reproduced like rabbits. Bruno was certainly right, at least in part, but Xavier couldn't see himself living in the countryside. Also, Bruno had his family with him, which was no longer the case for Xavier. Since his difficult divorce from Céline, there had been no other women, and he had joint custody of his eleven-year-old son, Olivier. When he presented this argument to his colleague, Bruno could only agree, chastened. 'Yes, you're right. It's more complicated for you,' he had admitted.

It seemed to Xavier that his life had gone off track at some point, and he had trouble pinpointing that particular moment. Often, he felt like a bachelor with no future, selling apartments to other people who were full of energy and ambition, so that they could build their lives there. These were the kind of plans that no longer seemed within his reach.

Nothing is really that complicated.

The things you perceive as difficult are most often just mental blocks. You're adding layers of unnecessary and unproductive anxiety.

Set them aside.

Nothing is especially complicated on board a ship, except when the vessel climbs up, then plummets down waves the height of a tall building, when seasickness strikes, and when a man suffers from claustrophobia. The captain of the *Berryer*, Louis de Vauquois, had been instructed by the Duc de La Vrillière to take great care of his astronomer. Guillaume Le Gentil wore a greenish pallor and a fixed stare whenever they ran into a storm. He said his prayers more often than the crew, but on a calm sea, on a sunny day, he was a delightful travelling companion indeed. The astronomer proved most useful, too: his precisely calibrated instruments provided the captain with measurements and information unmarked on his maps. Le Gentil plotted their course by observing the stars and the moon. On occasion, he succeeded in correcting the *Berryer*'s distance from land by several nautical miles. The great copper-and-brass telescope that he used for his observations, bright as gold on its tripod, had attracted Vauquois's admiration. Guillaume Le Gentil had invited him to put his eye to the small glass when the instrument was pointed at the full moon. What Vauquois saw took his breath away: the Earth's satellite loomed so large that its craters could be seen as clearly as the Saint-Malo lighthouse on his ship's return to port. On another occasion, the captain pointed out a streak of light in the sky that had been following them, to all appearances, for the past half-hour or more. Straightaway, Le Gentil fetched another telescope, shorter and thicker in diameter, standing on a single foot. The object was a comet, and squinting into his lens, the astronomer could just about make out its tail. For the next eight days, he busied himself with quill pen and compasses, darkening the pages of several notebooks in an attempt to calculate the comet's speed. The challenge filled him with delight, and as they approached the Cape of Good Hope, in fine weather, he forgot his fears of life afloat, even his seasickness. He took luncheon and dinner in the captain's quarters, feasting on succulent grilled fish unlike any in France. One morning, the *Berryer*'s nets even brought in a squid the size of a horse, with tentacles as long as the ship itself from prow to poop. The crew chopped it to pieces with their axes and the cook emptied an entire barrel of wine into several cast-iron cauldrons, so as to stew it in a heady *court-bouillon* of his own invention. That same evening, the entire company savoured the giant cephalopod's tender, salty flesh. The unexpected catch prompted tales of the terrifying sea creatures so often depicted in engravings, though it was never clear whether these were the fruit of man's imagination or a record of genuine sightings. According to the mariners, the strong currents and headwinds off the Cape of Good Hope sometimes gave a rare glimpse of the dreaded Caracac. The captain had never seen it, but he knew its description from the accounts of others. From his bookshelves, he produced a vast tome that must have taken the hides of a couple of fat sows for its binding, and opened it on a well-thumbed page. Guillaume Le Gentil bent over the book to discover a woodcut of a monster that resembled a scorpion fish as big as the *Berryer*. The creature's gaping jaws were easily five times the size of the great iron gates of Versailles, and from the top of its head a jet of water shot up like a fountain. The astronomer felt an icy shiver down his spine. If ever he crossed the monster's path, said Vauquois, in conclusion, he prayed God would come to his aid. Then he crossed himself and slammed the volume shut.

A few days later, Le Gentil stepped up to the bridge as the ship began its course around the southernmost tip of Africa. Standing close by the rail, he saw a great mass emerge from the waves, muscular, grey and gleaming, its skin tanned by the salt of the deep. A spout of water and air burst forth, rising to a height of fifty feet or more. Guillaume's heart stopped: the woodcut was made flesh. The Caracac was preparing to dive, and it would take the entire ship down with it.

He had never seen a whale, not even in a book, and now they surrounded the ship in great numbers, their blowholes spouting both to port and starboard, to the delight of the mariners who broke into hearty, rousing song. Reassured, Guillaume Le Gentil took a pair of steel-framed spectacles from his waistcoat pocket. They had been made to order by Margissier, who crafted all the lenses for his telescopes. The spectacles comprised two circles of ink-black glass, through which he could observe the sun with no risk to his eyes. He thought of Hortense, the wife he had left behind in Paris, who would have to wait for him for almost a year and a half. He pictured her in the silence of their lodgings, her slender fingers embroidering a delicate motif on a tablecloth, while his ship plied the waves with its escort of sperm whales. He was smiling at the thought of all he would tell her on his return, when a sudden gust of wind snatched the three-cornered black felt hat from his head. It came to land on the back of a nearby whale, from where, just as suddenly, it shot high into the air atop a powerful jet of water.

Xavier thought of her often. Nothing had worked with Céline. Could he ever have imagined that the wonderful moment of their first meeting would end, twelve years later, in court, with the decree absolute of a divorce judgement? Their story was just so ordinary, and it was this very ordinariness that made it all the more final. In its lack of originality there was no opportunity for a sudden change of heart. No, the banality of the statistics loomed large: one in two marriages end in divorce. The statistics were like a steamroller. A 50 per cent chance. Three years after a painful separation that had turned poisonous in its last few months, Xavier still found himself thinking about it several times a week. When the voice said: *If your thoughts are wandering, gently but firmly bring your attention back to your breathing*, he knew very well that such wandering would lead to the corridors of the Palais de Justice, to his lawyer, Maître Murier, and Céline's lawyer, Maître Guerinon, and to her friends' false testimonies, which described Xavier as a domestic tyrant who had Céline and their son living in a state of permanent terror. It would lead to the enormous demands of child support and his son, Olivier, whom Céline had full custody of that first year, and whom she had turned against him by telling him the divorce was all Xavier's fault. Bruno had been a great help during that difficult period, and a few good apartment sales at high prices had helped Xavier weather the storm. He had come out of it exhausted, but the seas were calmer after that, and he had managed to patch things up a little with Olivier. Xavier had made the decision never to speak badly of Céline in front of his son. This strategy of appeasement had worked in his favour, because Céline had relentlessly continued her character assassination of Xavier in front of the young boy. For a few months now, Olivier had seemed less susceptible to his mother's tactics.

The gong that signalled the end of the session chimed and Xavier opened his eyes. Sunlight flooded the sixty-square-metre apartment that he now called home. His job had helped with that, at least. He sold their 130-square-metre Haussmannian apartment in the best market conditions and used his contacts to find a quiet, well-located new one. There was one room for him, another for his son and a large balcony looking onto a courtyard that was usually deserted. It seemed to him that, in this life, nothing of significance would happen from now on.

Xavier got up from his chair and stretched. It was time to go to the agency.

Frédéric Chamois, his trainee, had received two phone calls. One was a request to view an eighty-square-metre apartment overlooking the courtyard, on the fifth floor with a lift – a good prospect that he'd had for sale for three months. The other phone call was from the new owners of the last apartment he'd sold before the noticeable recent decline in the market. Madame Carmillon had told him that a cupboard in the hallway hadn't been cleared by the previous owners. She had asked the agency to tell them to collect their belongings so she could use the cupboard. Having finished the refurbishments, the Carmillons had apparently just moved in.

'Did you complete the inventory of fixtures and fittings, Frédéric?' asked Xavier.

'Y-y-y-yes,' said the young man. 'I-I-I don't remember a full cupboard.'

'Me neither,' Xavier agreed. 'Oh well.'

Frédéric Chamois had a stammer. His stammer varied depending on the day and, mostly, depending on the rain. Xavier had noticed that 'Chamois' – he always called him by his last name – stammered less when it was raining. He had been very careful not to share that observation with him.

Xavier left the old owners a message. The following day there was no response, nor the day after. The contents of the cupboard must have been of no great importance, and Xavier was not surprised that there was no sign of life from the previous occupants. Once people have sold an asset, they don't like to return to it or hear any more about it. After they've cashed their cheque, they move on, forgetting even the face of the estate agent who negotiated the sale. Xavier's phone rang. MARCHANDEAU BANK appeared on the screen.

'Monsieur Lemercier, hello,' said his account manager. 'Are you in Paris, or overseas on business?'

'I'm in Paris, at my agency,' Xavier replied.

'As I suspected,' said the banker. 'Six hundred and fifty euros have been debited from your account, from Hong Kong. Your card has been hacked. I'll take care of it and I'll call you back, Monsieur Lemercier.'

'Pirates! Pirates! Pirates to starboard!'

Every man on deck interrupted his task to turn to the lookout boy. From his perch in a huge wicker basket just below the top of the mainmast, the boy's mission was to scan the horizon all around, using his spyglass to check the flags of ships passing near and far.

Guillaume Le Gentil hurried out of his cabin, clutching his great telescope and tripod. He trained the lens to starboard. In the bright circle of light he saw a ship emerge over the horizon, smaller than the *Berryer* but imposing nonetheless. Moving his lens up the mast, he saw the banner flying from the top: a skull and crossbones.

'They're manoeuvring!' the lookout bawled. 'They're coming straight for us!'

The captain stood beside the astronomer and extended his spyglass, scanning the horizon in his turn. Guillaume Le Gentil waited. A word of reassurance, perhaps, from the master of their ship. But Vauquois remained silent. He lowered his instrument and called out to his men: 'Half a point to starboard and hoist the mainsail!' The phrase was repeated instantly by the crew, and the ship turned sharply. Guillaume Le Gentil closed his eyes. His mind filled with images of cruel-eyed, gap-toothed men, their bodies covered in scars and tattoos. They would manhandle him, rip the silk and velvet from his back, throw his equipment overboard, then blindfold him and force him to walk the plank, out over the deep, in a hail of laughter, insults and spittle.

He would lose his footing on the plank and plummet into the icy, pitch-dark water. He could not swim. He would die of exhaustion in the immensity of the ocean, if the fish didn't tear him to shreds first. All for the vagaries of a heavenly body no bigger than a marble, that would cross the sun more than a year from now.

'We'll play the bastard a tune on His Majesty's pipes. Cannons to starboard side!' bawled the captain.

'Cannons to starboard!' hollered his men, in echo, and beneath their feet they felt the rumble of the huge guns, pushed into position by the crew in the hold. The shutters of twenty-five gunports clapped open all at once and the cannons' iron maws appeared, burnished bright from the damp below decks.

'We'll let him get a little bit closer,' said the captain, a sardonic smile playing at his lips. He took a clay pipe from his pocket and set about stuffing it, with an air of tremendous calm.

'Nothing like the smell of tobacco mixed with gunpowder,' he observed. Next, he struck an elegant, wrought-iron flint lighter, sending a cascade of sparks into the barrel of his pipe, which set the tobacco aglow. After a few puffs – an aromatic blend of spices and woodsmoke – he muttered: 'Monsieur Le Gentil, my most esteemed passenger, I suggest you cover your ears.'

The building was entered through one of those heavy oak doors which open with an electronic click of the lock triggered by the digital code. Behind the door was a foyer in the form of a broad passage leading to a courtyard, and on the right, the concierge's lodge. The passage was usually in darkness, and you had to find the light switch by feeling along the cool stone walls with your hands. It was an entryway typical of Haussmannian buildings which have kept their original door. Outside on the street, Xavier was waiting for his clients for their viewing of the fifth-floor apartment overlooking the courtyard. He watched the couples making their way across the small crossroads, waiting for one of them to come towards him: the Pichards. He had only spoken to them on the phone so far — in his line of work, you often didn't see people's faces until their first viewing. It was happening more and more. Email requests were increasing and everything was electronic. The sun was high in the blue sky and Xavier squinted and took out his Persol sunglasses, with their frames and lenses as black as ink. None of the passing couples approached him. He felt like a sentinel at the bottom of the building, of which he was neither an owner nor a tenant. He was just a passing man making a sale, taking his commission. He would never know the day-to-day life of this building, the neighbours, the co-op board meetings or the sun in the courtyard. There was a doctor on the second floor. He would never know the face of Dr Zarnitsky, GP, as indicated on the brass plaque which shone like gold in the doorway. He wondered how many times he had been stationed like this outside the entrance to a building, early for a meeting, with the apartment keys in his pocket and his information file in hand, standing all alone, like a lookout. It must have been hundreds of times. His profession was strangely intimate: selling an apartment or a house was a big deal. It was selling a piece of your life, a piece of your memories – sometimes even a whole life. It was closing a door that you would never open again. During the weeks or months their house was on the market, sellers would often reveal to him personal anecdotes about their lives, their parents, their wife or their grandparents. Generations passed, places changed hands, and often you would know nothing of the previous occupants. Xavier had recently read an article that had plunged him into confusion: apparently 85 per cent of people had no knowledge of their ancestors further back than 150 years. He had been struck by this statistic before realising that he too was among their number; here in 2012, he knew nothing whatsoever about his ancestors of 1862. Who were those people? No one in his family had ever mentioned them, and probably didn't know anything about them either – which made the figure of 150 years look optimistic.

A few months ago, he had found himself back at the edge of the neighbourhood, and it was only when he pushed open the entrance door that that he recognised it – the place had been one of his first sales. It was a good sale: a unique, 120-square-metre apartment in a 1970s building with an eighty-square-metre garden beyond the patio door. And it was all on one floor – a real find. It was certainly the apartment he had sold, but the owners were not the ones he had sold it to twenty years earlier. The apartment with the garden had come back on the market and come back to him. The cherry tree was still there, and the sellers had asked him to try a cherry – just like the previous owners had done. The fruit was still just as good, just as sweet. This same tree had continued its peaceful life, continuing to blossom while owners came and went. Xavier thought about telling them that he already knew the place, but in the end decided to keep the information to himself.

'Are you Monsieur Lemercier?'

He turned around.

The salvo's blast rang out like a great thunderclap. The cannonballs hit the water just short of the enemy's hull, sending up great sprays of water. The pirate ship showed no interest at all in what might come next; it made a sharp turn to the portside and sailed swiftly away. Guillaume Le Gentil had blocked his ears as instructed, but now he could hear a sort of high-pitched piping in his left ear, though no one was whistling nearby. He thought of his colleague Louis de La Marchandière, a renowned astronomer, who talked of nothing in recent years but the whistling he claimed to hear by night and day. He had ended his days in a lunatic asylum. But the affliction had struck when he was already well advanced in years, and somewhat senile, which was not the case for Le Gentil. The other, dreadful mishap was that his telescope had slipped from his grasp when the cannon blast shook the entire ship. Now there was a small dent in the tube. Guillaume checked Margissier's lenses straightaway, with trembling hands. Thankfully, everything seemed in working order.

Captain Vauquois had advised him to rinse out his ear with salt water and to remain lying down. Guillaume lay stretched out in his berth. *You are alive*, he told himself. *You are breathing. Everything is as it should be.* He felt the weight of his body, of his feet and hands, and he was mindful of the sounds all around him: the creak of timbers in the hull, the distant voices of the crew.

He closed his eyes. He thought of his Paris apartment, and pictured himself there, in such detail it seemed almost real. Here were all his books, his astronomical treatises. Here, he received eminent, elderly scholars. At thirty-five, he was as learned as a man twice his age, but with the fire of youth and the dreams that had carried him always onwards and upwards, from his first observations of the night sky at Coutances, in Normandy, when he was a small boy, to his Chair at the Académie des Sciences.

'My dearest,' he told his wife, 'a man who lives his passion is blessed by the gods.'

'Quite right, my darling,' Hortense told him in reply.

'Transit of Venus!' squawked a gravelly, piercing voice. Guillaume Le Gentil opened his eyes: Molière, the captain's myna bird, was perched on his bedside table and fixed him with an ink-black eye. Vauquois had determined to teach it a phrase connected with astronomy, in his honour. It had taken the bird barely more than a day to memorise the words, and it repeated them now at random intervals – as it would for the rest of its life. 'Transit of Venus!'

'Yes, the transit of Venus…' Guillaume sighed. 'Which last occurred one hundred and twenty-two years ago, and will occur next in one year's time, and then again eight years after that.'

'Eight years!' screeched the bird.

'Eight years…' sighed Guillaume, 'and then a hundred and five years more. In the years 1874 and 1882. After that, 2004 and 2012, and then 2117 and 2125…' and then Guillaume fell fast asleep.

The Pichards wanted to 'think about it' – which didn't sound promising. Xavier had been in the business long enough to be able to pick out the nuances of the end-of-visit conversation. 'We're going to talk about it' was better than 'We're going to think about it'. An 'I'll call you by tomorrow morning' meant the sale was as good as done. This visit had once again confirmed, as if confirmation were needed, the precariousness of the sales market. Xavier sat down at a café terrace and ordered a Perrier. That evening, Céline would come and drop Olivier off for the weekend. Their conversation would be very brief. You could always cut the tension with a knife, and the temperature seemed to drop ten degrees as soon as she rang the bell. Xavier needed to think of something to do with his son at the weekend, but nothing really came to mind, except perhaps a trip to Parc de Bagatelle to see the peacocks – but would Olivier want to see the peacocks? Xavier had always tried his best to be creative with his suggestions for spending time with Olivier. The idea of having a son glued to his tablet or to video games horrified him. Even though he had witnessed the dawn of video games with Pac-Man and Space Invaders, technology had given gaming a disproportionate place in the hearts and minds of today's children and teenagers.

'You can't spend your life in front of a screen! That's not living. I should know - I spend all my time in front of a screen,' he exploded at Céline one day. She was the one who had bought Olivier every app and tablet possible, seemingly with the sole aim of annoying his father.

'*I* spend my life in front of a screen. *You*, you do your viewings, you spend entire afternoons out and about,' Céline had replied, arguing that she couldn't do the same in her office, that at most all she could do was leave the building long enough for a cigarette break.

'My son is not going to become a mindless idiot playing video games. Life is museums, gardens, walks.'

The conversation grew more venomous and, in the end, Céline had simply hung up. She had reappeared the next day, expressionless, with Olivier in tow. Father and son had taken a boat out on the lake in the Bois de Boulogne. While he rowed, Xavier had had to respond carefully to questions like 'Why aren't you together? Do you love each other or not?' and 'If I wasn't here, you would never see each other again, would you?' Answering Olivier's questions required great tact; every single word had to be deliberated over before being spoken aloud.

Some evenings, Xavier called Bruno to talk. Bruno didn't have a solution and felt badly placed to give advice, given that he was living a wonderful life with his wife and two daughters. At least Bruno listened to him, which was better than nothing. He thought about calling Bruno now. He'd sent Xavier lots of photos of the work being done on the house. The new bed and breakfast was under construction in an outbuilding, and he was waiting for his friend to come and visit so he could show him his new life. He had made an Instagram account, a website, a Facebook page and a listing on Booking.com, and was pouring considerable energy into promoting The Dovecot. The most recent photo was of a basket of blackberries with the caption 'blackberries from the garden', followed by wink emojis. Bruno's life was now completely different to that of his former colleague. The photos had left Xavier nonplussed, but he sent back a smiling emoji, saying 'Well done, I'll come and visit soon.' But that was months ago.

His phone rang. Frédéric Chamois informed him that the new

owners were getting impatient about the cupboard filled with stuff from the previous occupants. 'I-I-I-I spoke to the woman, she's v-v-very annoyed,' Frédéric said.

'Okay,' Xavier cut him off. 'I'll deal with it.' The apartment in question was a twenty-minute walk from the café; he would go and take what he could or come back the next day with the car. It was clear that the previous occupants were not going to reply to his messages. It was up to him to load it all up and take it to the dump.

*

'I'm sorry for disturbing you, Monsieur Lemercier,' said the woman, who didn't seem at all sorry, but rather convinced of her right to demand the immediate clearing out of the cupboard in question. As Xavier had suspected, the apartment had since been refurbished; the office had been transformed into an open-plan kitchen living room, the old-fashioned ceiling mouldings had disappeared, and from what he could tell the kitchen at the end of the corridor had been converted into a children's bedroom. An aluminium scooter stood in the hallway. You saw it more and more in the city. Xavier found it irksome the way adults had patently appropriated what was a child's toy. With the greatest sincerity, they talked of how light and smooth it made getting around the city, without realising how ridiculous they sounded. Céline herself had dreamed of buying one for commuting to work.

'Here it is,' said Madame Carmillon, opening the much talked-about cupboard door with a flourish. The cupboard was hidden in the panelling of the wall and had a small key in guise of a handle. Xavier had simply not seen it. It wasn't even on the apartment inventory. It contained three ancient rolls of fabric, a vase, a broken barometer and a varnished, rectangular wooden chest, which must have been about five feet tall and a foot wide. It had leather straps held in place by large upholstery nails. Three old iron padlocks, opened with numbered codes, held it closed.

'It's mostly that,' said the owner, pointing to the chest. 'It weighs a ton,' she added. 'My husband has a trapped sciatic nerve from running. There's no way he could lift it, and neither can I.'

'I understand,' said Xavier, and he took the chest out of the cupboard. A ton was an exaggeration, but it weighed at least sixty pounds.

'I'll deal with the fabric and the old barometer,' Madame Carmillon conceded, appeased by having the estate agent at hand to deal with the matter immediately. 'But get rid of that chest, Monsieur Lemercier.'

The leather straps were carefully positioned to allow you to carry the trunk on your back, diagonally, like a hunter's rifle. Its weight was therefore spread over two shoulders, making the load much more manageable. Thus equipped, Xavier bade his old client goodbye and made his way back through the streets to the agency. At a crossroads, he passed a cellist who was carrying his instrument case on his back in the same way. The man glanced at him, then did a double take, no doubt wondering which instrument Xavier played.

'W-w-we don't know the codes,' said Frédéric.

'No, Frédéric, we don't know the codes,' Xavier agreed.

'Wh-wh-what could it be?'

The two men stood on either side of the chest, which was standing on the ground. 'We won't find out until we get the padlocks open, Frédéric.'

'We need an a-a-a-angle grinder to saw it open,' said the trainee.

'We don't have an angle grinder, and we're not going to buy one just for this.'

Frédéric's face lit up. 'We need a locksmith,' he said.

'Yes…' sighed Xavier. 'There used to be one around here, but he's gone.' They stood in silence for a minute. 'I'm going to go and see Claude,' Xavier decided. 'He might have an idea.'

The antiques dealer down the road from the agency had been there long before Xavier's arrival on the street. Contrary to what the name of his shop suggested – Smiles of the Past – its owner no longer smiled. His sales figures were in freefall; no one wanted snuff boxes, old corkscrews, vintage mercury mirrors, glass inkwells or rosewood bedside tables these days. These kinds of objects were of no interest to the new generation, and the few collectors who continued to bargain-hunt got them at rock-bottom prices on eBay. Claude was nearing retirement, and now spoke only of the olive trees on his property in the Mediterranean, where he planned to move the following year. He continued to open his shop every day to 'clock in', in his words.

'It's a trick,' he murmured.

'A trick?' Xavier repeated. The rectangular chest was now on the dealer's desk, and he was examining it with a jeweller's magnifying glass wedged in his right eye like a monocle.

'The codes don't do anything,' he said, 'the padlocks are useless. But they'd fool anyone. That must mean there's a secret to it... I don't understand why each padlock has a fleur-de-lys embossed on the back. Why the king's crest? Wait...'

He got up and took an old dip pen from the window display and resumed his work, scratching at one of the fleur-de-lys with the steel sergeant-major nib.

'Pass me the oil,' he said. Xavier passed him a bottle of gunsmith's oil, which he had taken out to polish one of the padlocks. The antiques dealer poured a drop onto a cloth, then wiped it over the royal crest.

'Got it!' he cried.

'You found it?' asked Xavier.

'The fleur-de-lys, they're the secret. They turn to the right.'

He used his thumbnail to spin the fleur-de-lys on the first padlock, and it opened with a click. He did the same with the other two, which clicked identically. The three padlocks gave way. He got up from his chair and opened the chest on his desk.

They were both silent as they looked at its contents.

'What is it?'

'A telescope,' breathed the antiques dealer. 'A very old telescope.'

It was long after nightfall, and a soft breeze played over Guillaume's face. He had positioned his telescope to the portside and aft, to observe the constellations of Centaurus, Circinus, Volans and the Southern Cross. With a yellow glass disc placed over the end of the telescope, the image was more sharply focused. He was comfortably installed in a blue velvet-upholstered cabin chair that he had brought on deck for the occasion, together with a rosewood side table and a crystal ink pot. With his goose-quill pen, he noted down measurements that appeared to correspond to his calculated estimates. The wrought-iron lantern hanging beside him swung gently, with a low creaking sound, then puffed out. Immediately, the ship's boy crossed to the where the astronomer was sitting, to relight it.

'Leave it, my young friend,' Guillaume told him. 'I've completed my observations for tonight.'

He shook a little blotting powder over the page to dry the ink, then blew on the paper and closed his notebook full of diagrams, sketches, figures and dates.

The ship seemed to float in the very darkness itself, the ocean indistinguishable from the sky. From time to time, the silhouette of a member of the crew passed by, lit by the flaming torches on the poop deck. A mixture of pitch and resin burned in great, octagonal glassed cages, like lanterns placed there by some giant Cyclops. The mariners seldom spoke to him – not that they felt any hostility towards his person, they simply had no desire to disturb him. His status as the ship's astronomer, and his royal mission, set him apart from the rest of the company. It had taken Guillaume a while to understand that the captain's men, even the highest-ranked officers, could not permit themselves to distract him from his thoughts, his observations and his note-taking. They would draw near, but stand a few paces off, waiting for the scientist to take notice of their presence and turn towards them, before greeting him and addressing a few words. They hardly dared cough to catch his attention. Guillaume told them often that they must not stand on ceremony, but the men of the *Berryer* refused to break the golden rule: never interrupt the astronomer at work.

Guillaume took a few paces around the deck to stretch his legs, then gripped the ship's rail and tried to make out the horizon with his naked eye. He saw nothing but darkness. He looked up into the night sky. The vault of heaven was covered with stars, and the night was so clear that he could see numerous constellations. He knew the strange, black star charts intimately. Each point of light bore a name. Suddenly, a bright streak shone pale mauve across an empty stretch of sky, and Guillaume stepped back in astonishment. More, infinitesimal gleams of light appeared. They glittered and sparkled as a burning wind set the torch flames flickering wildly. The sky glowed purple, in the dead of night, and the men of the ship hurried to starboard. Some muttered quietly among themselves, and the entire bridge seemed gripped with fear.

'Iron rain!' The lookout's voice rang from the top of the mainmast. The men exchanged glances and some of the crew crossed themselves. A glowing and yet sunless dawn was just breaking across the sea. A metal particle no bigger than a small slug bounced off the deck at Guillaume's feet. He bent to grasp it between his fingers. Twisted and still scorching hot, the tiny scrap of metal had crossed the universe to ricochet off the boards beneath his feet.

'Meteors,' said Guillaume softly. 'A meteor shower,' he corrected himself. He had read accounts of the phenomenon, which occurs when an asteroid falls through Earth's atmosphere, but he had never seen it other than in engravings. Sometimes the block of extraterrestrial ore fell to earth, or into the sea, in one piece. Unschooled, superstitious men called these 'thunderstones', because their fall through the atmosphere caused a break in the clouds and a reaction that produces a sound like thunder. Ancient druids and other wise men thought that the stones, which were far bigger than an ordinary piece of rock, were divine thunderbolts sent to Earth to warn mankind to mend its ways, or risk worse punishment in future. Alternatively, the mass would break up into tiny particles, creating 'Perseids', otherwise known as 'shooting stars' or 'iron rain'. A meteor shower. Such was this. The small fragments were falling continuously onto the deck now, while the sky filled with pale, purplish streaks not unlike the aurora borealis. Vauquois came and stood beside Guillaume.

'My men dislike this phenomenon. They say it brings bad luck. You are a man of science, Guillaume. Would you care to explain to them what is happening, in reality?'

Guillaume nodded.

'I am ever at your service, Captain Vauquois.'

'Gentlemen!' the captain called out. 'Our esteemed guest, a man who knows all there is to know about the stars and the planets, shall tell us the origins of the iron rain – lend him your ears!'

Guillaume did his best to explain to the company that the stars were like planets. They should imagine a small star falling like a vase toppling off a table and shattering on the floor.

'What you are picking up off the deck is stardust! These specks have taken millions of years to land at your feet. Keep them safe, give them as a gift to your wives and your sweethearts!' Guillaume was warming to his subject. 'They are the beating heart of the universe. See the sky and all its colours!' He swept the air with his arm. 'Behold, my friends, the work of God and the beauty of our world!'

The men listened, silent as a church congregation, nodding their heads. Captain Vauquois applauded his astronomer solemnly, and his men followed suit. Guillaume bowed his head in friendly acknowledgement. He turned and stood behind his telescope, while some of the men bent to pick up the scraps of metal that continued to fall with a soft tinkling sound. One struck the telescope's tube, producing a tiny spark and ricocheting off onto the deck. Guillaume started in surprise, then bent over his instrument: two small nicks in the brass formed a semicolon. He peered around, hunting for the miniscule meteor, then spotted it at last, caught between the ship's boards. He fished it out and slipped it into his waistcoat pocket. He would give it to Hortense.

The chest was divided into compartments, both large and small, all with straps holding various objects in place. The largest held the brass tube of the telescope, now tarnished to a drab shade like dark wood. In the compartment opposite, there was a tripod made of the same metal, which could be unfolded. The other compartments were filled with glass discs, some transparent, some in colours ranging from yellow to black.

'It seems to be intact,' said the antiques dealer. 'Where did you find this?'

'In an apartment,' Xavier replied.

'Do you want me to try and sell it for you?'

Xavier was quiet for a moment, and then smiled. 'No, I'm going to keep it.'

'You're going to spend your nights among the stars,' said Claude approvingly.

Xavier nodded, smiling. He now knew what he would do with Olivier that weekend.

*

The coffee-coloured window-cleaning fluid gave off an odour of ammonia. Xavier had found the bottle in the cleaning cupboard of his kitchen.

'If you clean it well, it should shine like gold,' Claude had told him. The antiques dealer was right. Xavier couldn't find a cloth so had opted instead for an old shirt that he had torn into four pieces. Now, the blue fabric was covered in black, and the copper of the telescope had begun to shine.

I'LL BE BACK TOMORROW; YOU CAN CLOSE UP THE AGENCY TONIGHT. THANKS, FRÉDÉRIC, Xavier had texted his trainee. The latter replied straightaway, asking what had been in the chest. The news that it was a telescope had not been greeted with much enthusiasm from Chamois, who simply replied OH...

Overheated from the exertion of cleaning, Xavier ended up taking off his own shirt. He took the telescope out onto the balcony and busied himself energetically restoring it to its former glory. He had almost finished the large golden tube and was finally looking at it in the sunlight, when he felt a small dent through the cloth under his fingers. He stopped and looked at what must have been the result of a blow to the instrument, which had knocked a cavity the size of his little fingertip into the metal. Another imperfection caught his eye; just above the dent, there were two small nicks in the shape of a semicolon. Xavier turned the telescope over and saw eight crosses, engraved with the point of a knife, or a nail file. They were all next to one another, forming a perfect line: simple marks in the shape of St Andrew's cross. The eight marks didn't seem to refer to any astronomical pattern. They had been incised into the metal of the telescope by the hand of a man who was without a doubt the only person who understood their meaning. Xavier picked up his cloth again to tackle the eyepiece at the base of the tube, where the observer would place their eye. The sleeve of his old shirt, now covered in black tarnish, revealed the shining copper beneath, and what looked to be an inscription. Xavier put down the cloth and went to find his glasses to take a closer look – over the last five years, his vision had deteriorated drastically, and for months now he had been holding books or files further and further away from his face in order to read them, before eventually putting on the reading glasses that he had bought in the neighbourhood pharmacy. It was indeed an inscription, in elegant engraved letters:

GUILLAUME LE GENTIL, BY ORDER OF THE KING.

'What are you doing, my friends?'

'We're fishing, sir,' the head chef answered with a broad smile. The chef, a fat man with a blond ponytail, had prepared the plumpest, most succulent fish Guillaume had ever eaten, every day since they had set sail from France.

'But I see no lines?' said Guillaume.

'No indeed, sir!' he smiled. 'Just these huge nets. Missed him!' he called out to one of the men, who shrugged his shoulders helplessly.

'They're too quick for us, Master Cockerel!' said the ship's boy.

'You'll bring me in fifty of them! And stop complaining,' retorted the cook. All the crew called him 'Master Cockerel'. The term came from the Latin *coquere*, to cook, vulgarised as 'cockerel' in the parlance of the sea, but which was nothing whatever to do with a farmyard rooster.

'But… they're flying,' Guillaume observed quietly, as he stared at the surface of the water.

'Of course they're flying! Doesn't our astronomer know a flying fish when he sees one? I'll prepare you one with garlic you won't forget!'

The silvery fish, similar in its shape and size to a mackerel, bore two side-fins shaped like wings. They raced just beneath the surface of the water, then shot up and flew for a good few seconds in the air, like a bird gliding with wings outstretched, before sinking beneath the waves once more. Clouds of them flew in formation before Guillaume's eyes. The men of the *Berryer* were trying to catch them in nets attached to handles as long as the branch of a tree. They weren't the only ones attentive to the flight of these astonishing fish. Frigate birds were flapping all around the ship and diving into the airborne shoals with their beaks wide open, to catch and swallow them whole. One of Master Cockerel's commis chefs had armed himself with a blunderbuss which he reloaded regularly with sawdust and rock salt, firing salvos at the birds from the weapon's trumpet-shaped barrel. None was hurt, but the blasts kept them briefly at bay, so that the men with the nets could continue their task.

'Bring me a fish!' cried Master Cockerel.

Straightaway, one of the men plunged his hand into a barrel and brought out a winged fish which he placed on a wooden platter to be carried with deference to the ship's cook.

'Take a look at that, sir,' Cockerel said to Guillaume. 'You'll never see its like in France.'

Guillaume bent over the fish, its gills still palpitating. Delicately, he unfolded the huge, translucent fins that served as the creature's wings.

'Truly the work of God, sir, as you said on the night of the iron rain.'

'Indeed... You're right, Master Cockerel. God is in all things.'

The ship lurched suddenly, sending the wooden platter flying out of Guillaume's hands. The fish was tossed overboard, and Guillaume watched as it spread its wings above the surface of the water, before diving down.

'God has seen fit to save His creature,' he said.

'True enough, sir,' said the cook.

'Thank you for showing it to me, Master Cockerel.'

''Tis all the science I have, sir – I know the beasts of land and sea, and I respect them.'

'You're a good man, Master Cockerel.'

'As are you, sir. Your very name proclaims it. Le Gentil!'

Guillaume smiled.

'Who is Marie?' asked Guillaume. Master Cockerel glanced down at his powerful, muscular forearms, each one broader than the astronomer's thigh.

'My beloved,' he said, with a sigh.

'A most beautiful thing, I find,' said Guillaume.

'What, sir?'

'For a man to ink the name of the woman he loves into his own skin for life. Do you think I should tattoo the name of my true love into my arm?'

'Sir!' cried the cook. A gentleman of your standing does not wear tattoos.'

'Yes,' Guillaume nodded. 'If you say so, Master Cockerel.'

The cook took a tiny meteor from the pocket of his leather apron.

'As you suggest, I shall take my Marie a speck of stardust. I'll have it set in a fine brooch and she shall wear it in her hair.'

Guillaume Le Gentil was a well-known figure, it seemed. The internet had informed Xavier about the epic saga of the astronomer who braved all dangers, in the end never to observe the transit of Venus. Destiny had made a mockery of the scientist so many times and with such imagination that his story, if it hadn't been true, could have passed for an ironic fable of misfortune. The astronomer had written a book in two large volumes, each hundreds of pages long, about his adventures: *Journey through the Seas of India, by Order of the King, at the Moment of the Transit of Venus across the Sun*. Xavier had ordered himself a copy online.

He returned to the telescope, which had now been carefully cleaned and was gleaming on the balcony. The sky was blue, only a few clouds lingering above the rooftops which hid the sun, and there was no daytime moon to be seen. He twisted the wheel on the tripod to turn the eyepiece towards him and find out whether the telescope still worked, 250 years after its manufacture. He put his right eye up to the small brass ring and closed his left. The first thing he saw was the rooftops of Paris, and a woman on her balcony. The lenses were easy to adjust using the notched disc on the side, just within reach, and the image quality was high. The woman was a few streets away from Xavier's apartment, and with the naked eye he wasn't sure he could have even made out her outline amongst the mass of zinc roofs, chimneys and electrical antennae that covered the buildings of the city. The telescope had an incredible range, and Xavier felt as if he was watching a neighbour, ten metres or so away, on the other side of the courtyard. Her mid-length brown hair was blowing in the wind, and she was leaning on her wrought-iron balcony seemingly lost in thought. She must have been in her forties, around the same age as Xavier. In her left hand she held a white rectangle which he couldn't quite make out, but which seemed to be a sheet of paper. She had that focused, faraway look that smokers often have when they're taking a drag of a cigarette, leaning on the balcony railing with a blank stare and a mysterious smile on their lips. Except she wasn't smoking. She slowly began to tear up what must have been a letter. The white shreds scattered in the wind. She turned around, went back inside, and closed the window, disappearing into the semi-darkness. Xavier stayed there for a few moments, unmoving, his eye glued to the brass ring, but he couldn't make out her silhouette inside. Nothing. She lived on the fifth floor; it must have been divided into two apartments, because there were flowers on the other side of the balcony, geraniums and pink lilacs. Xavier had noticed that in Paris, if someone liked flowers, they would put them on all their balconies. On the dark-haired woman's balcony, there were none. He lowered the telescope and discovered a thirty-something man on the floor below, wearing a sky-blue shirt with his tie undone. He was smoking and talking on his phone. Presumably that apartment had been converted into an office, and the man was an employee on his break. Xavier moved the lens and his gaze fell upon the nearest roof, where some workers were in the process of restoring the zinc. The small blond worker was clearly in disagreement with the tall bearded one, and both men seemed annoyed. Was it a personal dispute? Or perhaps an argument over a goal in a recent football match? The blond suddenly put his tools down ten metres away from his colleague and turned his back on on him. The other man shrugged his shoulders. Xavier turned towards a chimney several buildings away. A pigeon perched there took off, only to be replaced a second later by another bird. Xavier adjusted the lens. The bird was marbled with brown and had blue-tinged feathers. It looked around before taking off itself, spreading large, pointed wings, nothing like those of a Parisian pigeon. A common kestrel. The majority of them lived on Notre-Dame or the Sacré-Cœur, venturing out to neighbouring areas to hunt.

He looked back up to the sky, and his circle of vision filled with a light blue. At that moment there was nothing astronomical to see with the telescope. When Céline brought Olivier over that evening, he hoped there would be a crescent moon and some stars. His knowledge of astronomy was rudimentary at best; a vague memory of Ursa Major – with its shopping-trolley shape – and some other stars whose names he didn't know. He would have to revise the basics of the subject before showing the telescope to his son. He glanced at his phone on the coffee table – no messages – a sign that nothing important was happening at the agency.

Imagine you are in a place where you feel comfortable. A place you know. Or an imaginary place.

Visualise it clearly. Turn your head to the left, to the right. Look in front of you.

Stretched out on the sofa, his headphones on and his eyes closed, Xavier pictured the background of his computer screen at the agency – a beach with fine sand and palm trees – that he had downloaded from the numerous wallpaper options available on the internet. He didn't even know where this seashore was. Far away, in any case. Far from the beaches of France. Sometimes he lost himself in the image for a few moments during the workday. Now was the time to enter the scene, following the voice's instructions.

Become fully aware of your surroundings. Slowly pay attention to the sounds, the temperature, the light.

And Xavier started walking along the beach.

The sand was fine and silky as flour, and the water was blue like the turquoise gemstones a jeweller had shown him once, near the Académie. He removed his silver-buckled black leather shoes, then his stockings, and felt the soft, burning sand yield to the tread of his bare feet.

*

The *Berryer* had made land the day before. Time for Guillaume to take his leave of Captain Vauquois and his men. Far out in the eastern Indian Ocean, Isle de France was the first port of call on his voyage to Venus. From here, he would take another ship to his final destination, Pondicherry, on the south-eastern coast of India.

'It has been our honour to have you on board. I wish you good fortune in your observations of the heavens,' said Vauquois.

'Transit of Venus!' squawked his myna bird. Guillaume smiled and bade farewell in his turn, to the captain and crew. The men carried his possessions – chiefly trunks of clothes and specially made cases for his instruments – to the residence allocated him by the island's governor.

The governor of Isle de France would receive him that evening. Meanwhile his aide, Amédée, a thin youth with a close-shaven head and no wig, and who had served in the king's navy, showed him around his lodgings, on the second floor of a fine clapboard mansion painted pale blue and white. The building was flanked by broad balcony terraces. Guillaume's apartments consisted of three large, sunlit rooms, each opening onto the next. Their windows, and even the four-poster bed, were hung with delicate tulle drapes that floated on the air and were intended to protect against insects and their bites. A large bowl of unfamiliar, exotic fruits awaited him, together with a harpsichord. Amédée presented a well-built man with bronzed skin, by the name of Toussaint: he would assist Guillaume during his stay on the island, and would, he said, be 'always close to hand'. Guillaume bowed his head in greeting, and the man did the same. Neither of them spoke a word.

'I'll unpack my clothes,' Guillaume ventured.

'Ah, no!' Amédée was firm. 'You are a gentleman of the Académie. There are people to take care of that.'

Amédée would always address him by his official title, 'Monsieur l'Académicien'. Already, Guillaume yearned for the *Berryer* and its crew, who had never referred to him as anything but 'Master Astronomer'.

'Perhaps, *Monsieur l'intendant du Gouverneur*,' he said, 'but I prefer to see to it myself. No one else adjusts my telescopes, no one else hangs up my shirts and waistcoats. In another life, I had thought to enter the priesthood, and a man of God – like a soldier – takes care of his own belongings. The habit has never left me.'

'I understand,' said the steward, quietly.

'I do have one request,' said Guillaume.

'Granted, *Monsieur l'Académicien*!'

'I should like to visit one of your beaches. I've heard they are most beautiful; but I have only ever seen them engraved in black and white.'

Amédée nodded. 'It is high time you saw them in colour, sir.' He turned to Toussaint, who smiled.

'You have been a long time at sea. I'll take you to our most beautiful beach.'

*

Dazzling blue. Everything was blue, and the water lay as still as the sky. Until now, the only beaches Guillaume had known were those facing England, along the north-west coast of France. He had gone there as a child, and later in his youth, with his family. Windswept dunes dotted with clumps of grass, and the immensity of the sea, more often than not coloured deep blue with a hint of drab yellow-brown, and rolling waves that threatened anyone who stood too close and was careless of the undertow. The tide would retreat almost to the horizon, and they would tread the expanse of rippled wet sand and silty pools with frozen feet, to reach the icy water's edge, then wade further still to stand barely thigh-deep. But never more than that. No one knew how to swim. Everyone took the greatest care. Then the wind would get up, the clouds would turn hostile, like the waves, and they would hurry home.

'Such beauty…' said Guillaume quietly to himself as he walked on the sand. He marvelled at everything around him. There were the strange trees he had seen in engravings: long tube-like trunks which grew outwards in a curve, with pointed leaves right at the top like an exploding firework of greenery. The local people called them 'palms'. They lined the strip of white sand, which was so hot and bright in the sun that he had to squint, and wished he had brought his black-tinted spectacles. A gentle, warm breeze caressed his face when he turned to face the ocean. It was truly the exact colour of the gemstones the old jeweller had shown him. He felt hot and pulled off his wig, with its tight rows of white curls. He ran his hand through his hair and walked to the water's edge. He saw multicoloured fish circling – yellow, pink, blue, white. Large grey boulders stood at the edge of the lagoon and Guillaume climbed up onto one of them while his protector looked on in amusement, arms folded across his chest. Sitting astride the rock, Guillaume stretched his arms wide as if to embrace the sky and sea. The scene was like an illustration in a book of exotic travels. It seemed to him to be paradise on Earth. All that was missing were the animals one sometimes saw depicted. Almost imperceptibly, the rock shifted, then rose. Guillaume clutched at its surface and leaned forward to discover that the round boulder had grown feet, and even a head, which was now turned to look at him – a head that looked for all the world like an elderly snake, wrinkled, sage and with a serene smile. Guillaume slid and tumbled backwards onto the sand as the giant tortoise ambled away to the trees.

'Are you all right, Monsieur?' his watchman was kneeling beside him.

'Perfectly fine,' said Guillaume with a smile, as he dusted himself off. 'I thought a tortoise was no bigger than a man's hand!'

'Oh, these are aged, aged creatures,' the other replied, as he helped the astronomer to his feet. 'They are two or three hundred years old.'

'Three hundred years,' pondered Guillaume. 'They must have seen four or five transits of Venus... I should love to bathe in the water,' he sighed, gazing at the sea.

'But you must, Monsieur.'

'I cannot swim,' replied the man of science, sadly.

'I can. I'll help you.'

The telescope turned out to be an excellent way to spend the evening. The ancient artefact, which seemed straight out of a Jules Verne novel or a Tintin comic, had immediately captivated Olivier. In the hour before his arrival, Xavier had tried to learn a little more about the world of astronomy. He had already located Cassiopeia, Ursa Major, Ursa Minor and of course Venus, the planet that shone the brightest after the moon, and whose radiance outstripped all the other stars. Luckily, the moon had emerged after dark, and a good two-thirds of its surface shone over Paris like a lightbulb in the black sky. Father and son had installed themselves on the terrace for a dinner of croque-monsieur, Olivier's favourite dish, with his favourite dessert, the croque-banana – a sweet croque-monsieur with banana, to which Xavier added chopped glacé cherries. When the croque-dessert was ready, he dusted it with icing sugar. They chatted about what Olivier had done with his mum that week – among other things, dinner at Céline's sister's house with her daughter, Emma, who was fifteen, and whom Olivier described as 'ugly and stupid'.

'You shouldn't talk about your cousin like that,' Xavier objected. 'She's not stupid.'

'But she is ugly,' said Olivier. 'You said she's not stupid, but you didn't say she's not ugly.'

Xavier was caught out as usual, and managed to say: 'She's a teenager, so she's not very graceful at the moment, from what I've seen in photos.'

'Emma's always been ugly,' Olivier insisted. 'Hasn't she?' he asked his father, lifting his head from his croque-banana.

'Okay fine,' sighed Xavier. 'Your cousin is ugly and that's all there is to it.'

'Aha! You see!' Olivier exclaimed triumphantly.

'Are there any pretty girls in your class? You mentioned a Louise once?'

'Yeah, Louise is pretty,' Olivier mumbled, and his father realised he would get no more out of him.

'Pretty how?' he tried.

'Pretty like… pretty,' Olivier said evasively.

Once the digression on beauty was concluded, they finished dinner with their ritual; a glass of amaretto for Xavier, with two ice cubes and a slice of lime, and a glass of almond syrup for Olivier, also with two ice cubes and a slice of lime. He wasn't allowed alcohol, of course, but he had fallen in love with the smell and taste of amaretto when his father had allowed him a tiny sip of the amber liquid one night – 'Don't tell Mum, promise?' So, Xavier had gone in search of almond syrup, which hadn't been at all easy to find. Luckily, an Italian manufacturer had put his wares online, and Xavier regularly ordered syrup from him in packets of six. The syrup was the same colour as the real amaretto, which made the effect all the more attractive for Olivier, as, after diluting it with water, he had the feeling of drinking much more than his father.

'Can we look through the telescope?' Olivier asked impatiently. He had only been allowed to put his eye to it to look at a single star before dinner. Xavier had told him the story of its discovery in a forgotten cupboard in an apartment he'd sold, and then the story of the man for whom it had been made.

'He never saw the transit of Venus?'

'Never,' Xavier replied. 'But he had a very long and very enjoyable journey, and he saw other things: oceans, panoramic views, sunsets. He went to places that hardly anybody would have been to. Nowadays, with the internet, magazines and adverts, we've all seen pictures or videos of the other side of the world, where we will never go. But in his day, there were no pictures. You had to go there. It was like going to the moon,' Xavier concluded dreamily.

'So shall we look at the moon?' asked Olivier.

'Yes, let's! Here we go!'

Olivier settled himself on a stool and Xavier on a folding chair. He pointed the telescope towards the heavens, adjusted the lens, then swung the telescope towards his son, who put his eye to it.

'Wow! It's so close!'

Xavier smiled – he had done well this evening.

'You can see loads of craters.'

'Those are impacts,' Xavier said with authority. 'Big meteorites which struck the moon a long time ago.'

'Did they explode when they hit?'

'Yes, they exploded. There was a huge bang, and lots of flames and dust.'

'Wicked,' said Olivier.

'If you go slowly to the right, you'll see a really bright star – yes, just like that,' Xavier said, watching as Olivier carefully manoeuvred the telescope. 'Do you see it?'

'Yeah, it's really bright, and it has a little shining circle in the middle.'

'That's Venus,' said Xavier. 'The planet that our friend Guillaume Le Gentil, the true owner of our telescope, never managed to see pass across the sun.'

'And it passes across every one hundred and twenty-two years?' asked Olivier.

'Yes, two pairs of transits eight years apart, separated by gaps of a hundred and five and a hundred and twenty-two years.'

*

Olivier was sleeping now, and Xavier gently closed his bedroom door. Strangely, he wanted a cigarette. He used to smoke a packet of gold Bensons a day, long ago. After multiple attempts to quit which ranged from patches to nicotine gum via simple cold turkey – and never lasted more than five days – he had tried a meditation program which had worked. The female voice had helped him concentrate on his breathing and his thoughts, and, more specifically, to let the desire to light a cigarette and inhale the blue smoke pass him by. The voice was right: the craving for a cigarette didn't last more than six minutes; then the brain moved on to other things. That evening, the unexpected craving disappeared after barely thirty seconds. The telescope was still on the terrace, and Xavier lowered it to look at the buildings once more. The telescope's field of view fell on the window of the woman on the balcony. The window was dark, as were all those around it. Then suddenly it lit up, and Xavier blinked. It wasn't the light that made him blink, but what he saw through the window: a zebra was standing on four legs in the living room. Motionless, the animal seemed to be watching him, its head turned towards the glass. Xavier took a step back, gathered himself for a moment, and then put his eye to the telescope once more. The zebra was still there. A female figure, dark-haired and naked, walked past it, and then the light went out.

A yellow spider was picking its way over the topmost keys of the harpsichord. The creature's spindly legs extended almost from the tip of Guillaume's thumb to his little finger. Like an autonomous hand with impossibly slender digits. Watchful and alert, it stopped dead in its tracks as Guillaume placed his hands over the lower keyboard to play the first counterpoint of Bach's *Art of the Fugue*. After the first few notes of the celestial, sparkling piece, written as if to converse with God himself, the arachnid continued its slow progress, and Guillaume watched with a smile.

The harpsichord was a little out of tune; doubtless it had suffered in the heat and humidity here on Isle de France. What was it doing here in his apartments? He wondered briefly if it had been placed there for his enjoyment, as a courtesy, though he could not remember telling anyone he could play, during preparations for the voyage. The melody rose to heaven, regardless, a reminder of that other life, which had lasted quite long enough. His family had destined him for the priesthood, and he kept the memory of the infinite quiet of the cloister at dusk, a sense of peace that he had never truly recovered since – except once or twice, in his observations of the Milky Way. The smell of incense, too, remained profoundly connected with his years at the seminary and his communion with a God depicted as tradition dictates, first up among the clouds, then coming to Earth and dying on the Cross in the body of Lord Jesus Christ. One of his finest moments of 'communion' with the divine had occurred when the cathedral organist in Coutances gave him leave to spend an afternoon at the keyboard. Guillaume had played alone for more than four hours, and it had seemed as if his hands were guided by some higher force, a force that would watch over him forever, a source of the unconditional love he had never found among his fellow humans. A few months later, astronomy had assumed a greater importance in his life than he could ever have imagined. That first meeting with his master, Joseph-Nicolas Delisle, had changed everything. He would never be a priest, nor a monk, still less a cardinal, let alone pope; he would be an astronomer.

'You can stay – listen, it's very beautiful!' The spider shifted its legs cautiously, seeming to hesitate at the scientist's suggestion.

The night before, Guillaume had dined with the governor of the island, Antoine Marie Desforges-Boucher, and had presented him with a small spyglass made by Margissier, whose new-fangled lenses afforded a magnification eight times greater than a conventional instrument. The governor had insisted on showing him his collection of butterflies and moths. A seasoned mariner, he spent his time on land catching Lepidoptera. He would put them to sleep with potent fumes of distilled rum, then delicately pin the rarest specimens. Guillaume marvelled at the iridescent wings that shone like blue enamel on metal.

The governor told him their name: blue morpho butterflies. 'Toussaint will take you to a forest where they spiral in the air in their hundreds, all around you. A prospect that is sure to delight you, *Monsieur l'Académicien*.'

They ate civet of boar. The dark flesh must have stewed for hours over a gentle heat, it was so tender, with a delicious, smoky flavour. The governor explained how these familiar creatures had come to so distant an island. The Dutch had introduced them in 1606, during their rule. Hundreds of boar had been brought by ship, and only nine had survived the voyage, but they had reproduced at an alarming rate. A century later, the population was out of control, and the incessant destruction they wrought had forced the island's French rulers to take action. Hunting was universally permitted, and the numbers of wild hogs had now dropped to acceptable levels. The governor seemed genuinely concerned by the business of the boar that had so preoccupied his predecessors. He seemed equally interested in the true distance from the Earth to the sun – the object of Guillaume's mission to observe the transit of Venus. They discussed the moon, and the tides, and the importance of mapping the world as accurately as possible, for military and humanitarian purposes alike.

Guillaume had retired to his bedchamber and written a letter to his wife. He had taken out his quill pen and his crystal ink bottle, and lit a candelabrum on the balcony.

> My dearly beloved Hortense,
>
> I am surrounded by beauty, but it is yours I desire most. I have a rendezvous with a planet that bears the name of the Goddess of Love, but it is you I wish were beside me now on this great balcony in the warm night air. As you know, my fellow astronomers are journeying to the eclipse from around the world, a good hundred of us or more, each making his own way to meet with Venus. I pray I do not disappoint His Majesty the King, and that I shall take the most precise measurements possible. I have been told that all ships to Pondicherry are confined to port due to political difficulties in the region, and that the English have gone to war against our troops. Hence, I shall map the island while I wait. I find the most astonishing seashells; I think I shall classify them for the museum. I shall bring you the first one I collected. I wish I were a painter, to record the things I see, which are beyond any picture I know. I am at the very centre of our world, in the middle of nowhere, and everything seems to me like a

dream. There are boar just like the ones in the forests of Normandy. I picture you working at your embroidery, your hands so delicate, and my longing for you knows no bounds. How lonely I feel at night, without you; how cold the sheets when I slip between them and fall asleep dreaming of your face… I see it, your dark hair and your pearl-like complexion. I know the perfect oval of your cheeks, your smile, I know the shape of your pretty ears, the elegant arc of your nose and the light in your hair spread loose over your shoulders. The skin of your body, speckled like the constellations in the map of the stars. I could name each one. You are my heaven, my only star.

Guillaume

He had sat for a moment before the finished letter, then held it close to one of the flames on the candelabrum. The paper caught fire, and he held it for as long as he was able, before dropping it into a small glass bowl, where it burned itself out.

*

Deep in thought, Guillaume reached the final notes of the first counterpoint in *The Art of the Fugue*, the ones that leave the piece as if unfinished. Like *The Art of the Fugue* itself. Bach's riddle, left for the world to solve. He turned and watched the spider walk away, towards the balcony, across the wooden floor.

Xavier looked again as soon as he woke up the next morning. The dark-haired woman's window was ajar, and there was no zebra in the apartment. He immediately searched HALLUCINATION on the internet and found the following definition: A HALLUCINATION IS DEFINED IN PSYCHIATRY AS THE EXPERIENCE OF SENSORY PERCEPTION WITH NO IDENTIFIABLE STIMULUS; FOR EXAMPLE, SEEING OBJECTS THAT AREN'T PHYSICALLY THERE, OR HEARING VOICES WHEN NO ONE IS SPEAKING. This mention of voices when no one was speaking led him to the idea of meditation. Spending half an hour with the voice, and being still – not watching beautiful strangers through the window with the telescope or seeing zebras in apartments – would be the best way to clear his mind. Olivier loved doing what he called 'a voice session' with his father from time to time. The two of them lay down on the living-room rug, side by side. Xavier placed his phone between them and put it on loudspeaker.

He opened the app to find that its icon had changed overnight. Xavier tried to find his usual program with the female voice, but it had disappeared. New meditation programs were available now.

'The normal voice isn't there,' he told his son.

'It doesn't matter,' replied Olivier. 'Let's choose another voice.'

Xavier was disappointed; he was used to hearing the female voice, a faceless voice that always repeated the same soothing phrases: 'Make yourself comfortable… concentrate on your breathing… leave your thoughts aside…' Never again would he hear that voice say those words. Sometimes he found himself wondering who the woman was, imagining her. She had vanished in the millions of web hits a minute. The website had seemingly wanted to tidy up their offer, suggesting new content with new recordings. After the divorce Xavier had spent a long time alone, during which the very idea of a new romance was inconceivable to him. Bruno had tried to introduce him to women – usually his wife's friends. It never worked; he always ended up talking about his divorce, custody, and the thousands of worries caused by this rupture in a life that had once seemed all planned out. These rendezvous were more like impromptu therapy sessions for two than the first exciting moments of a burgeoning love. The following year, Xavier had had a fleeting, casual dalliance with the new florist on the street. After a few months, when Xavier had begun to wonder seriously if they could build a future together, she had announced one evening that she had reconnected with her childhood sweetheart on Facebook and that she was leaving to join him in Brittany. The shop had closed. Now it was a shoe shop. Xavier fell once more into a well-advised solitude.

'Her flowers were rubbish, anyway. They wilt after three days!' Bruno tried to reassure him, grouchily. Since then, there had been no one; no dates, no flirtations.

The little gong sounded. Olivier and Xavier closed their eyes.

Make yourself comfortable, began a man's voice.

Guillaume took from his pocket the beautiful seashell he had collected after his first swim, assisted by Toussaint who had supported him under his belly and taught him the breaststroke. They had gone back to the sea several times since, and tried other beaches, but that one was still Guillaume's favourite. He learned to swim, not as well as Toussaint, who was taller and more strapping, but at least now he could float in the water without fear. He could even swim out slowly at a tangent to the beach, towards a rock or a buoy. By way of thanks, he had invited Toussaint several times to observe the Milky Way, the moon, the stars and even a comet, through the telescope.

He had collected a *Cypraea tigris* shell as big as a chicken's egg, oval and bright as glazed porcelain, its speckled surface like leopard skin. Guillaume carried it with him everywhere, like a talisman. He was careful not to break it by slipping as they walked down a forest track. Guillaume followed Toussaint to a clearing indicated by the governor, to see the blue morpho butterflies. They had come once before, but Toussaint reckoned their first visit had been too early in the season. There would be many more now.

'Toussaint,' said Guillaume, 'I've been here for four months now, and we see one another almost every day. I should like to ask you something: I call you Toussaint. Please call me Guillaume. We should address one another simply, like friends and equals!'

Toussaint turned to face him, smiling, but a shake of the head signalled his refusal.

‘I beg you, call me by my name!’ Guillaume insisted.

‘Guillaume…’ said Toussaint, walking on ahead.

‘You see, Toussaint, you spoke it out loud, here in the forest. The animals are our witnesses, and so it shall be from now on!’ Guillaume was delighted.

They walked in silence for a time, before the astronomer spoke again:

‘Perhaps we shall never see one another again in this life, once I have left Isle de France for India. We should seal our meeting, our friendship, by addressing one another by our first names. Friends and equals! Like Our Lord Jesus Christ to the faithful.’

‘You speak such fine words,’ said Toussaint. ‘Like a preacher.’ He turned around. ‘Thank you for your friendship, Guillaume.’

‘Thank you, Toussaint.’

They walked on.

‘Toussaint?’

‘Guillaume?’

‘The bird that has vanished, the dodo…’

‘Yes?’

‘You know this island like the back of your hand. If there were any left, surely you would know where they might be. I should so love to see one!’

Toussaint stopped in his tracks and turned slowly towards Guillaume. A silence fell between the two men, and Toussaint seemed to hesitate.

‘I cannot say where the dodo is. Only saints and madmen have the right to see it. Unless… If you confide a great secret in me, I can confide that secret in you.’

Now it was Guillaume’s turn to hesitate. They stood in silence, and the sounds of the forest rose all around, the distant cries of its furred or feathered inhabitants, no one could ever be sure which. Then Guillaume sat down on a bank nearby.

‘My name is Guillaume Le Gentil de La Galaisière. You are right, I speak like a priest. I wanted to enter the priesthood, in another life.

I'm thirty-five years old today. I have a wife, her name is Hortense. She lives in France. I think of her often, I talk to her, I write to her. She never replies… because Hortense does not exist. She is my own invention. An imaginary woman. I have never had carnal knowledge of a woman's body. I spent years at the seminary, training for the priesthood, and then I turned to astronomy, and time passed, and Hortense, whom I invented in my youth, lived on with me. Perhaps I might meet a real woman, but the thought scares me. Too much time has gone by. I prefer my Hortense.'

Toussaint watched him in silence then nodded slowly.

'You are a saint. And a madman. Follow me, Guillaume.'

They branched off their path and climbed for a good thirty minutes to the highest part of the forest. Toussaint stopped to listen, then cupped his hands around his mouth and blew four long hissing sounds. Four identical sounds answered him immediately. He turned to Guillaume:

'You must never tell anyone what you have seen.'

Guillaume nodded.

'Never. Even if I come to write my memoirs one day.'

They entered a clearing. An old man was sitting on the ground. His skin was even darker than Toussaint's. He held a stick in his right hand. Toussaint walked across to where he sat, then crouched and spoke in a language Guillaume did not recognise. The man opened his eyes, and Guillaume saw that their irises were pale, grey and opaque like waning, gibbous moons. He was blind. The man nodded, then struck the ground repeatedly with his stick, as if sending a coded signal. Toussaint returned to Guillaume's side.

'He is the keeper of the last dodos. A very wise man,' he added, in respectful tones.

The rapping ceased, and Guillaume turned his head to catch a deep, clucking, rasping cry.

Dohhh-dohhh.

Two birds came towards them, moving slowly and hesitantly. Their large feet seemed seemed to wobble as they touched the ground. Each was a good three feet tall, and their plump bodies were covered in grey-blue plumage. Their hooked beaks, yellow at the end, were easily the length and breadth of a man's hand. One of the birds planted itself right in front of Guillaume and looked up at him with small, bright yellow eyes.

'Dohhh-dohhh', said the bird.

'Dodo,' Guillaume replied.

'Only four remain,' said Toussaint, 'and no females. What you see before you, Guillaume, are the last specimens in the history of the world.'

Guillaume nodded slowly. The keeper signalled to them, and they squatted down beside him. The old man spoke a few words in the island language. Toussaint translated:

'He asks you to give him your hand.'

Guillaume held out his hand, and the old man took it in his. He closed his eyes then looked up. His milky-white pupils were just visible. He whispered again.

'He says you will go on a very long journey. But the thing you seek is not what you think.'

Guillaume frowned. 'Tell him I am looking for Venus. A planet in the heavens.'

Toussaint translated the astronomer's reply, and the old man shook his head, then smiled and answered in his own tongue. 'He says that you have travelled very far in search of something that was right before your eyes, and which you hold in your heart of hearts,' said Toussaint. He went on: 'You are not seeking after a planet. You are looking for love. You will find it at your journey's end.'

Xavier was bent over his copy of *Journey through the Seas of India, by Order of the King, at the Moment of the Transit of Venus across the Sun on the 6th of June 1761 & the 3rd of the same month 1769*, which had arrived that morning. The two-volume book was unique, because it was in fact a facsimile of the 1770 edition, with its eighteenth-century type. Here and there, a lower-case 'f' replaced the letter 's', like a kind of visual speech impediment on the astronomer's part. Xavier felt as though he was diving into a magical grimoire, full of twists and turns, meanderings and discoveries in wondrous lands.

That morning, he had eaten breakfast on his balcony and again pointed his telescope towards the far window, to check there was no black-and-white-striped member of the horse family beyond the windowpane. The dark-haired woman had appeared several times, but Xavier could only make out her silhouette. She had opened the window, a phone pressed to her ear, and seemed upset by the conversation, checking her watch before hanging up. He had seen her pick something up – a bag, or a piece of clothing. She went out. Xavier mentally counted the time it took her to go downstairs – he was well positioned to make a guess, having gone up and down his own stairs plenty of times. He wasn't wrong: the door to the carriage entrance opened and the woman came out onto the street. She was wearing a black skirt, a vest top and ankle boots and was walking in the direction of the café on the corner. She waited at the pedestrian crossing for the lights to change, then headed for the terrace, greeting a brown-haired man who was already sitting there. He stood up at her arrival but did not kiss her. Xavier was so focused on them he let his coffee go cold. He would have loved to have been able to read their lips. The two spoke without looking at each other. A waiter approached and she shook her head – a sign that the conversation wouldn't last long. There was a long silence between them, then the man seemed to become agitated, counting things known only to him on the fingers of his right hand. The woman shrugged her shoulders and silence fell once more. Finally, she placed her hand on his, in a gesture of appeasement, but while shaking her head in such a way that implied there was nothing to be done. The man lit a cigarette and threw his head back. The woman said a few words to him and then stood up and left without looking back. She crossed at the traffic lights and walked towards her apartment building, entered the code, and disappeared through the door. Xavier pointed the lens of the telescope towards her window, five floors up, and saw her appear in her apartment a few moments later. Her silhouette came into view for a moment, disappeared, then returned to the window and opened it, leaning on the balcony, a mug in hand. Xavier refocused his view on the man at the café; he was still there. He took out his phone, smoking his cigarette in an engrossed manner, and typed in a number. Xavier returned to the woman on the balcony. She turned her head and looked back indoors – surely at the ringing of her phone, which she had left on the table. She paid no attention to it, looking once more over the city. The man hung up and put his phone down on the table. He signalled to the waiter to bring him a coffee then picked up his phone again and tapped in a number. On the balcony, the woman didn't move; he was calling someone else now. Whoever was sitting next to the man would get the whole story. As it happened, there was a free table next to him.

'Yeah, yeah… I know… it is what it is. Maybe it's better this way,' the man said into his phone. Xavier had sat down at the next table and ordered a coffee. He had put on his shoes and socks as quickly as possible, not even stopping to comb his hair, and had strode hurriedly towards the terrace.

'It's not working out… we're too different,' said the man, who had now put on dark glasses to protect himself from the sun. Xavier drank his coffee, half feeling as though he was in a remake of *Rear Window* by Alfred Hitchcock – in which he had somehow stolen the role from James Stewart – and half feeling that he was just a lonely, bored loser who spied on the break-ups of faraway, unknown neighbours. He was vacillating between Hitchcockian romance and urban misery when the man said:

'What's going to become of her? Nothing! Nothing! And I don't care! Alice can go about her business with her zebra. She'll end up living with it!'

Xavier lifted his head from his coffee. He was almost tempted to place his hand on the man's forearm and say: 'Sorry to interrupt, but I need an explanation. Who is this woman who lives with a zebra in her apartment? I want an answer and I want it now.' But he did nothing. The man cut the conversation short after looking at his watch and realising he was late. He hailed the waiter, left some coins, and got up, disappearing into the boulevard. Xavier recapped the information to himself: she was called Alice, she had just broken up with the man in the dark glasses, and she lived with a zebra in her apartment. His phone rang and CHAMOIS appeared on the screen. He picked up.

'Yes, Frédéric?'

'Hello, a-a-are you not at the agency?'

Xavier looked at his watch. His James Stewart impersonation had taken much longer than he thought.

He went home to take a quick shower, brush his hair and shave, before going to meet his trainee. Passing through the hall, he picked up his package containing the two volumes of Guillaume Le Gentil's memoirs.

It was all quiet at the agency that afternoon, and Xavier could continue his reading. He was at the point where the astronomer had left Mauritius aboard the ship *La Sylphide* and was heading for the Indian coast of Coromandel, when the door opened.

'Hello,' said a woman's voice, and Xavier looked up from his book to see the dark-haired woman apparently known as Alice. She stood before him, dressed the same as she had been this morning, in her black skirt and vest top. Xavier was immediately seized with panic. Had she seen him watching her with the telescope? What was she doing there? What was this sudden intrusion into his reality?

'I live in the neighbourhood,' she began, 'and I would like to put my apartment up for sale. Would you be able to give me a valuation?'

'Yes…' replied Xavier, blankly.

'My name is Alice Capitaine. I live at 18 Rue de la Pentille. When can you come?'

Xavier looked over at Chamois, who nodded.

'Now, if you like,' replied Xavier.

He walked down the street by her side, suspended in that strange moment where both people are waiting for someone to break the silence. Xavier stole a glance at her. She had a beautiful profile; the sunlight picked out the elegant outline of her nose and her brown hair. Xavier noticed some beauty spots on her neck, whose positioning reminded him of the constellation Ursa Major.

'Have you lived in the neighbourhood long?'

'Yes, I was born here, and I've come and gone ever since.'

'And you want to leave again?'

'Maybe. Or maybe not,' she said, thoughtfully. 'I could stay in the neighbourhood, but on another street. I often pass by your agency, and, you know how it is, one day you just decide to push open the door,' she said, smiling.

'Why my agency?'

'You're the closest, according to the internet.'

'I see,' said Xavier.

They stopped at a pedestrian crossing and Xavier looked at the table on the terrace where he had sat by the man in dark glasses. It was now occupied by two tourists who had put their suitcases at their feet and were presumably searching for their Airbnb on their phone. Alice didn't look towards the terrace. She entered the building code and the carriage door opened with a click.

'It's about sixty square metres, or sixty-five, I don't know exactly, and I have a balcony that looks towards Montmartre, which can be seen from far off.'

Xavier almost corrected her, telling her that the balcony on which he had observed her looked towards the south, and therefore not towards Montmartre. They got into an old lift, and she pushed the number five. The two of them were silent in the two-metre-square space, and as the lift went up, Xavier could smell a perfume emanating from her, which he identified as verbena. There were two doors on her floor, the one on the right belonging to the owner who had put the flowers on their balcony. Alice took out a bunch of keys and opened the door on the left.

'Please come in,' she said, and Xavier entered a small room with dimmed lights. She had placed small frames on the walls, which held metallic-blue butterflies. Alice headed towards the living room, and Xavier followed in silence. He entered the large room that he had seen from his window. There was a curved nineteenth-century sofa with dark mahogany scrolls, and other pieces of furniture scattered around, a tasteful mixture of old and new, and accent lighting spread about to compensate for the lack of a ceiling light in the centre of the room. A large round glass table was covered in tools, fabric and at least twenty bottles of various sizes, which at first glance gave the impression that this part of the room was sort sort of workshop, where extremely precise, delicate things were crafted. He turned around and nearly jumped out of his skin: the zebra. It took up the entire space between the wall and the door. It was really there, with its striped, shiny coat and its head turned to the left. Perfectly still.

'Sorry,' smiled Alice. 'I'm a taxidermist.'

Xavier approached the animal. Its muzzle was uncannily realistic; he was almost expecting to see it flare its nostrils and shake its head.

'It's an order for a client,' Alice continued. 'This zebra was stuffed more than a hundred years ago. He wanted me to restore it because it's starting to spoil. The only solution was to install it in my apartment. Normally I work for the Natural History Museum. Can I show you around?'

Xavier nodded. 'I'm going to measure the living room,' he said, retrieving a laser pointer from his pocket. He stood next to the zebra and pointed the laser at the wall, then did the same from the window to the door.

'The kitchen,' Alice said, opening a door.

'You don't have an open-plan kitchen,' noted Xavier.

'No, I must admit I've never understood the appeal of having a washing machine in the middle of the living room,' Alice said drily.

They moved into the corridor.

'My bedroom,' she said, pushing open a door, and Xavier saw a bright room with a copper-framed bed, shining like Guillaume Le Gentil's telescope.

On the wall there were posters from the museum, detailing exhibitions from years ago, as well as a large wardrobe of light wood, burnished by the years it had served as a closet.

'It's nice and light in here,' Xavier commented, before pausing in front of a painting of two silky foxes in an almost abstract landscape. The name of the painter was written in large letters: Yamaguchi Kayo. 'It's beautiful.'

'Yes,' said Alice. 'He was a very famous Japanese painter. In his whole life he only painted animals.'

They left the bedroom and Alice opened another door. 'My daughter's bedroom,' she said, and Xavier saw the typical decor of a bedroom belonging to a girl of around ten years old.

'How old is she?'

'Eleven,' Alice replied.

'My son is the same age,' he said, with a smile.

'What's his name?' asked Alice.

'Olivier – what's your daughter's name?'

'Esther.'

'Esther's room is almost as big as yours,' Xavier commented, his gaze falling on a shelf piled high with various objects ranging from miniature perfume bottles to anime girl figurines. In the middle, mounted on a golden rod atop a wooden pedestal, was a stuffed flying fish, its transparent wings outstretched.

'It's my daughter's prized possession.'

'Did you make it?'

Alice nodded.

'A few years ago, we read a story where the heroine saw flying fish, and it wasn't long before I heard "Mum, bring me a flying fish",' she said, smiling.

The bathroom was a good size, and next to the walk-in shower was a small window which looked over the city.

'I'll show you the other balcony,' said Alice, closing the door.

They went up a few steps and entered a small room filled with shelves, whose windows opened onto a balcony with a view over the roofs of the city, and the Sacré-Cœur in the distance.

'It's very unusual,' Xavier said, admiring the view in the afternoon light. 'You must get magnificent sunsets.'

Alice smiled. 'Yes, we've had some beautiful ones. Esther's favourites are pinned up to the right of the window.' Xavier turned towards the wall and saw pictures of the view, all the same, but where the sky was sometimes orange, sometimes pink, sometimes a glowing red.

'We take them on my phone, and I print some of them out.'

Xavier nodded. 'It's full of charm, this apartment,' he said, before taking out his laser pointer to measure the room with the sunsets. 'It's between sixty-five and sixty-seven square metres, but I need to measure precisely to be sure. You have the lift, the shops nearby and it's in a pleasant neighbourhood. Now, in 2012, we're at around 9,000 euros per square metre. If we base that on sixty-five square metres, it's worth 585,000 euros.'

Alice nodded. 'Thank you.'

'If you'd like to put it up for sale, my assistant will take some photos and I'll look after the rest.'

There was a silence and she looked towards the window.

'Either I find an apartment with a terrace in the neighbourhood or I leave… maybe to go far away. I have an offer to take my work overseas.'

'Far away?'

'Washington,' Alice said.

'That certainly is far. And your daughter?' he asked.

'She would come, we've talked about it.'

Xavier didn't dare ask what would happen with the girl's father in this case.

'I have a question,' he said, and Alice turned to look at him. 'At the museum, is it possible to visit the taxidermy workshop? I think my son would be fascinated by it. You see, I'm always on the lookout for new things to do with him on the weekend. I only see him every other weekend,' he added, as if to justify himself.

'I understand,' said Alice. 'Technically no, there are no visitors, unless you know someone who works there.' There was a pause, then Alice added: 'Come this weekend. Esther will be there too. I'm working Saturdays at the moment. I'm late on a dodo.'

'A dodo?' Xavier asked, confused.

'The extinct bird,' Alice smiled. 'I'm restoring one.'

On the way back to the agency, Xavier noticed he was walking much more slowly than usual. The streets and the boulevard went by in a sort of haze, as if viewed through one of those frosted windows sometimes found on the doors of old apartments, behind which you can see only figures and guess at the size of a room and its furnishings. Alice and her apartment. Just Alice. Alice. She gave him a feeling of déjà vu. Of course, déjà vu because he had seen her through the lens of Guillaume Le Gentil's telescope, and the impression was surely no more than a strange trick of the mind, and yet he felt there was something else, something undefinable. As if he already knew her, as if he had already met her. He wondered if they had been at the same school or the same college; if this feeling came from the limbo of childhood, long forgotten. But no, he had never had a classmate called Alice Capitaine. He'd never even met an Alice before.

Guillaume screwed the polished glass to the end of his telescope so that he could adjust his optical settings, as he did every week. The surrounding vista disappeared, leaving a blur in which he could still see the tall, shadowy mast of the *Sylphide*, and the silhouettes of a handful of the crew. Four weeks aboard ship and the monsoon wind was seriously hampering their progress towards India. The day they set sail, he had watched the shoreline of Isle de France disappear into the distance, with a strange apprehension that things would not go as planned. A great deal of bother and business had attended their departure, for weeks on end. The situation in Pondicherry was unclear: some said that the French fort had fallen to the English, others that it would fall soon, and still others besides that the English would never kick the French out of Pondicherry. He must meet his appointment with Venus at all costs. It was set for 6 June, and now there was no time to lose. On arrival, he must train his telescopes and set up the camera obscura that would project the image of the sun and the tiny marble crossing its surface onto a white-painted wall, in real time, like a shadow play. He had dreamed of the two discs – one of light, the other dark – for so many nights!

Guillaume turned the little wheels to achieve the perfect focus on his polished glass disc. He tightened two screws to fix the focal point, then removed the disc and stowed it away with the other ten, in their large case. There sat the final disc: black as ink, the only one that allowed him to observe the sun without burning his retina. Carefully, he removed it from its soft leather pouch. He sat down on the deck of the bridge, held the glass to his right eye and closed his left. Everything disappeared. Guillaume turned his head to look up at the sun. There it was, pale and visible as the full moon on a clear, starry night. Hortense, he whispered to himself, tell me what I am doing here, in the midst of the seas of India? A gust of wind sent the spray splashing up over the ship's rail. He felt its cold saltiness on his face and lips.

'Is everything to the satisfaction of His Majesty's Envoy?'

Guillaume removed the black disc from his eye and saw the ship's captain. 'His Majesty's Envoy' was the preferred term of address on this ship. Guillaume got to his feet.

'It seems to me that we are losing speed,' he said.

The captain looked vexed. He smoothed his white wig.

'I cannot tell a lie,' he said. 'The monsoon wind is stronger than expected, and if things do not improve…'

'If things do not improve?' Guillaume repeated his words.

'I will not risk the ship, or my men. We will not carry on to the coast of Coromandel but will turn around and sail back to Isle de France. That said, His Majesty's Envoy should rest assured, the weather may yet improve and the monsoon wind may drop. I've seen it many a time!'

'Well, I have not,' breathed Guillaume. 'There is only one transit of Venus. The next is in eight years' time.'

And the one after that more than a hundred years from now.

Xavier chopped up the peppers, then the basil leaves, with the porcelain knife that he had bought the week before. He grated the piece of parmesan he had purchased at the Italian grocers. A solitary meal, one he had eaten many times before. While he was waiting for the water to boil for the spaghetti, the radio, which he had tuned to France Info, returned to the recent election of François Hollande and his statement of 'I, president,' which he had repeated fifteen times in three minutes and twenty-one seconds, during the space of which he detailed the plans he would put in place if he were elected. Journalists had got their hands on the exact name for this figure of speech – anaphora – and they were hungrily dissecting it to work out exactly what awaited the country in the next six months. Xavier turned the radio off.

At the end of the afternoon, he had searched in his apartment database for something to present to Alice Capitaine. She had told him that she could pay more than the price of her own. The eighty-square-metre apartment on the courtyard was clearly too expensive; there were two others that she might like, but they had no terrace and no real balcony that looked over the city – let alone the equivalent of the sunset balcony, or Xavier's own terrace. It was aggravating. Xavier dropped the spaghetti into the boiling water and the strands spread out like pick-up sticks before he could push them below the surface, tapping them with a wooden spoon. Seven minutes to wait.

He laid the table on the terrace with his plate and cutlery next to the telescope. Alice's window was lit up, but she had drawn the net curtains, and he hadn't seen anything through them since he had pointed the telescope in their direction half an hour earlier. Why did she want to sell that apartment, which was charming and seemed perfectly suited to her and her daughter? Sometimes people want to rid themselves of an asset because it has too many memories. The past builds up and in the end it takes over the present, until one doesn't know where one is or where one is going – a decision is made, and often a radical one. The person must move on, quickly and callously, like a lobster tearing itself away from one of its claws during a fight, in order to flee and save itself. The claw takes a long time to grow back – but grow back it will.

The timer rang. Xavier drained the pasta in a sieve before returning it to the pot to dry off a little, and then serving it with the mixture of peppers, basil and parmesan, drizzled with olive oil. It was pretty good, but it was missing something. One more ingredient and the recipe would be perfect.

Was she divorced, or married? She hadn't mentioned a man. Generally, one always finds a way to let slip the information that one shares one's life, to discourage potential advances or misunderstandings. She hadn't. Xavier had typed her name into the internet and found an interview she had given in the workshop of the Natural History Museum, to a specialist wildlife magazine. A photo accompanied the article. It showed her from a distance, surrounded by colleagues, all dressed in lab coats and busy working at tables covered in bottles and tools whose purpose Xavier didn't know. Alice's worktable had on it a curious small rat, identified as *Allactaga major*, which Xavier would have described as a cross between a mouse, a kangaroo and a rabbit. It was frozen in a pose worthy of a Walt Disney cartoon and seemed to be smiling at the camera. Still unfinished, its body was covered in tiny golden pins that made it look bedecked with jewellery. In the interview, Alice described her profession with grace and modesty; she spoke about the beauty of the beasts that taxidermists tried to preserve for eternity and said that the endeavour was entirely unselfish. On the contrary, it was an exercise in sharing, so that humans could understand that nature, and the different beings that surround them, all live in the same world; a fragile world which must be respected. None of the animals was the product of hunting – they had all died of natural causes and lived their whole lives in nature reserves regulated by the Washington Convention on Animal Protection.

Xavier had tried to enlarge the photo of Alice, but the site only had a small-format image. Next, he had typed ORIGINS OF THE NAME CAPITAINE, which took him to a genealogy site whose goal was to make an inventory of all the surnames in France and divide them by region over more than a century. He learned that the name 'Capitaine' belonged to only 3264 people born in France since 1890, in 88 *départements*. The highest concentration of Capitaines lived on the tip of Brittany, mainly in Finistère and Morbihan. Xavier thought of the port of Lorient, where Guillaume Le Gentil had embarked on his search for the eclipse of 6 June 1761. He cleared the table, put the dishes in the dishwasher, and turned it on. *Journey through the Seas of India* was waiting for him on the bedside table. Before opening the book and finding Guillaume in a bad way, heading towards the first eclipse, Xavier poured himself a whisky – Bowmore, no ice – and inhaled its peaty scent. When Bruno had been at the agency, they'd kept a bottle there and would drink a glass of it together to celebrate a good sale. He should call Bruno, faraway in the Dordogne with his bed and breakfast, The Dovecot. Time was going by. Xavier took a sip of whisky and stretched out fully dressed on his bed to resume his reading.

The monsoon had lifted. The *Sylphide* couldn't reach India before the transit of Venus. The captain of the frigate ship had just decided to turn back.

My dearly beloved,

I am quite literally all at sea – our frigate has just begun manoeuvres to turn around and sail back to Isle de France. The wind is strong and the waves are huge. I can scarcely put pen to paper. I will not be able to observe the transit of Venus from Pondicherry, which remains the very best vantage point. We are far out in the ocean, with just two days until the eclipse. There can be no question now of setting up the camera obscura to watch the transit projected against a wall. I shall have the large, fifteen-foot telescope set up, secured with the four lengths of wood I made sure to bring along with me.

Still, I feel my mission is slipping through my fingers. I pray to God. And to you, my dearest one.

My love, my Venus. My eternal eclipse.

Your beloved,

Guillaume

The deck pitched in the hot wind, and Guillaume watched as the men busied themselves on the portside quarterdeck, fixing a mast with a halyard to secure the huge telescope that he had assembled himself, kneeling to screw the three tubes together. The crew were in no way concerned with Guillaume's astronomical observations, but the turn of events seemed to bother them greatly, nonetheless. His Majesty's Envoy was their passenger and succeeding in this mission would be an honour for the *Sylphide* and her crew – yet it now looked so unlikely. A big man with a shaved head – the best on board for knotting ropes, Guillaume had been assured – was applying himself to the task with care and precision. He pulled on the ropes, thick and thin, and tied them with the dexterity of a fairground conjurer, his huge hands suddenly deft and supple as a ferret. Soon, he had lashed the telescope to the mast. The captain bawled the order for the ship to remain stationary in the water, aligned with the sun as instructed by Guillaume. A man fetched a wooden armchair and set it down heavily, level with the telescope's eyepiece.

'Pray His Majesty's Envoy be seated.' He invited Guillaume to adjust the height and position of the seat on the deck. Guillaume sat down and put his right eye to the telescope.

'Just right,' he said.

A bare-chested man wearing a leather apron knelt down and opened a satchel to produce four huge iron nails and a cast-iron hammer that Guillaume would have been quite unable to lift. He set about nailing the astronomer's chair into place so that it would not slip. Each hammer blow drove the points of the nails through the chair's clawed feet and into the boards of the deck.

Pouring with sweat, the man stood up.

'It will hold now, sir,' he assured Guillaume, who thanked him for his work.

Four men lifted the great telescope up over their heads as best they could while the ship rolled, and Guillaume tried to frame the sun in the large black disc that he had placed over the eyepiece. At last, he glimpsed it in the black circle, but it disappeared almost immediately.

'Lash me!'

The rope man came to Guillaume's side.

'What do you mean, sir?'

'Lash me to the telescope. I can't hold it steady in this wind, it's too heavy.'

The man stepped back and thought for a moment.

'How much do you weigh?'

'One hundred and fifty pounds, I believe,' said Guillaume.

'The weight of a small calf,' said the man, still thinking hard and frowning.

'Position yourself as you desire, and then stay still.'

Guillaume leaned in to the eyepiece.

'There,' he said.

He heard a rope pass over his head with a sound like the crack of a whip, then another around his torso. A third circled his arms. Meticulously and with astonishing speed, the sailor tied him to the telescope with a series of fiendishly clever knots pulled so tight they might be soldered joints of steel.

Fifteen sailors surrounded Guillaume, now lashed to the telescope. One of them held the astronomer's pocket watch close in front of his face. Guillaume's eye darted back and forth, from the watch to the telescope's eyepiece.

'First contact should have begun,' he muttered.

Silence.

'The watch is slow!' he cried out. 'And I cannot get the sun in my sights in this swell. I cannot do it,' he gasped. 'Untie me. We'll try another way.'

Guillaume saw the rope man's great hands fluttering all around him. He was released. The huge telescope swung around and almost knocked him senseless as he bent down towards the deck. The men caught it in the nick of time.

'Do you have any hourglasses?' Guillaume asked the captain.

'Four!' came the reply, and the captain yelled to the ship's boy to fetch them immediately.

'I shall try another telescope,' said Guillaume. 'We'll use a table, and one of the men will turn the hourglasses over on my signal.'

'Table!' cried one of the crew, and another man dived down into the hold. A table was produced along with the hourglasses. Guillaume extended his brass telescope. There was no time to nail the latest piece of furniture to the deck: the men would have to hold it fast with their bare hands. The heaviest of them all was ordered to sit on the tabletop with the hourglasses. Guillaume fixed the sun in his sights and for a few seconds, he glimpsed a small black sphere that had just made its appearance, before the eyepiece slid to the right.

'Hourglass!' he called out, and the boy who had been dispatched to fetch them turned the first one over.

For a good hour or more, the young sailor flipped the hourglasses on Guillaume's orders, like a showman tricking his audience with upturned cups. Guillaume would catch the sun in his sights, only for it to disappear once more. Sometimes he even lost sight of the small black marble that was Venus, though he knew it must still be there. Then the wind rose and the sun disappeared behind the clouds. Guillaume set down the telescope. A long silence fell over the bridge. The crew stood stock-still. A fine drizzle began to fall, and someone handed Guillaume a three-cornered hat. He looked around at the sailors who stood gazing at him, not daring to speak.

'Gentlemen, I thank you for your steadfast help,' he said in a pale voice. 'The observation has not been a success.' Guillaume got to his feet and shut himself in his cabin. Three hours later, when he had not emerged for dinner, he heard a knock at his door. The captain entered without a word. He placed a bottle of whisky and a silver goblet on the table.

'For our finest moments, and our saddest. It helps, at times,' he said quietly. 'I bid His Majesty's Envoy good night.'

Xavier sat at the terrace of a neighbourhood café, having ordered a cocktail he hadn't drunk for over twenty years: a Bloody Mary. The tomato juice, vodka and tabasco, with a dash of celery salt, would bring this day to a close. The afternoon was turning out very differently from his usual schedule of viewings; in the morning, in front of the mirror of his bathroom cabinet, he had even trimmed his rogue strands of hair with the office scissors. He had also shaved twice, put on a white shirt with cufflinks which he rarely wore, brushed his jacket and polished his black Oxford shoes. He had thought of Bruno, who, if he had been there, wouldn't have missed the chance to make fun of him: 'Where are you going, man? Got a date with a princess? Selling the Château de Chambord? What's her name?' But Bruno wasn't there any more, and Xavier had to admit it: he missed him. The agency was more fun with Bruno exclaiming 'Who was that jerk?' once an irritating client had left, or asking anyone who would listen if they had thought to ask for the name and, more importantly, the phone number of the pretty postwoman. Bruno must be living the dream in the Dordogne, spending pleasant days with his family, full of plans for his bed and breakfast, debating wallpaper colours for a future room with his wife, Charlotte, or discussing once more the layout of the rockery in the landscaped garden. Yes, Bruno had made the right choice in leaving the city, along with its cars that reproduced like rabbits. His life was probably just like a family advert from the 1980s, in which the mother and father had breakfast with their children in the mornings, in the courtyard of a beautiful, sunny house, sharing hot chocolates and piping hot coffee, laughing all the while. Usually, these ads were extolling the virtues of a chicory brand or an insurance policy. But in just twenty seconds, they were able to depict a disconcertingly simple kind of happiness that Xavier had never felt was within reach. Bruno, on the other hand, had clearly managed to achieve it.

Alice Capitaine had arrived at the agency wearing a long, beige dress and semi-tinted sunglasses. Xavier had picked three apartments in the neighbourhood to show her, all within walking distance of one other. Admittedly, none of them had a terrace looking over the city, but they had courtyard balconies, and one even looked over an interior garden. With these viewings, Alice would see for herself the current real estate offerings within her budget. She liked the layout of the first apartment – large rooms and a bedroom for her daughter, as well as a kitchen at the end of the hallway — but its position on the ground floor worried her. The second, with the large balcony overlooking the interior garden, was deemed too small, although the balcony and its view over the trees on this beautiful day was certainly an asset. The third, devoid of any balcony where one could spend time with a cup of tea or a glass of whisky, was refurbished to a high standard. Every aspect had been carefully considered, from the dressing room to the bathroom. However, it had an open-plan kitchen in the middle of the living room, and Alice, in her words, didn't want to 'see the washing machine three metres from my Louis XVI chest of drawers'. Xavier had pointed out that for a reasonable price, the kitchen could be dismantled and rebuilt in its original place, which was currently presented as a 'small office'.

'Really, what I need is the first apartment but on a higher floor, with the balcony of the second and the dressing room of the third,' she said to him, as they walked down the street. 'I'm sorry,' she added, smiling. 'You must see people like me all the time.'

'No,' replied Xavier. 'I don't see people like you all the time – I mean, people don't often articulate their needs so clearly,' he added, because his first, spontaneous answer, seemed to him a little over the top.

'To be honest, the apartment I'm describing is just a fantasy, of the kind we often make in taxidermy.'

Xavier turned to her with questioning eyes.

'Some clients want an animal that has never existed, so we make a rabbit with wings, or a swan with a duck's body. I don't like doing those,' she added. 'They are selfish projections. Fantasies.'

'And… your zebra?' Xavier replied.

'He's fine,' said Alice. 'I've finished him, and he'll go back to his home.'

'To his owner?'

'Exactly, to the house of Luigi di Lugano. He's Italian, a very particular man. I'd have trouble guessing his age – eighty, maybe more, maybe less. He is passionate about science and exploration; he has an incredible library. He's one of the most scholarly people I've ever met. I always tell him he's the last Renaissance man. He loves that.'

'What does he do?' asked Xavier.

'I've never known what his profession is,' Alice replied. 'He doesn't seem to have any financial limitations. He lives in a townhouse with five floors and a garden, right in the heart of the Marais. An asset like that must be worth…'

Xavier finished her sentence: 'Between six and eight million euros.'

'Far from what we're looking for,' Alice concluded with an air of melancholy.

'You must meet some interesting people in your profession,' Xavier said.

'You too, no?'

Xavier shrugged. 'Less than in yours, I reckon.'

They continued to walk, this time in silence. They passed a café with a terrace, and Xavier almost asked her if she'd like to sit down and have a drink, but he didn't dare. Something was going on here, something beyond her obvious charm. He had a peculiar sensation of déjà vu, but bringing it to her attention with the clichéd, 'I have the feeling we've met before,' wouldn't lead to anything, he was sure of it. Worse still, it might seem like a clumsy attempt to come on to her.

'Washington,' said Xavier. 'Are you seriously thinking about it?'

'Yes, they want an answer in less than a month. There are times like this in life where you have to make a decision that could change the next twenty years. It's not easy.'

'I understand,' Xavier replied. They arrived at the crossroads, near the café where he had watched her with the man in the dark glasses. This time, the table was occupied by two Asian tourists who were looking at the boulevard and the passers-by, smiling. They had probably just landed in Paris after a twelve-hour flight and were savouring the moment.

'I'm going home,' said Alice. 'Thank you for showing me those apartments. If you find anything else, don't hesitate to let me know.'

'I won't,' Xavier promised.

'And do come to the museum next Saturday, I'll let security know.' They shook hands and Xavier watched her walk away towards the carriage entrance.

Xavier shook the bottle of tabasco over his cocktail and took his first sip. For the first time in a long time, he felt happy for no reason. An idea was taking shape in his mind. A crazy idea, perhaps, but maybe that was the spice of life. The apartment Alice was looking for fit the description of his own apartment exactly.

When Guillaume woke, it was a few moments before he realised that it not been a bad dream. He had indeed failed in his observation of the transit of Venus across the sun. The whisky bottle was half empty, but his head felt fine. Sunlight filtered through the canvas curtain over the porthole, and the ship seemed motionless. He rose from his berth, dressed and went out onto the bridge without his white, rolled wig. The light was dazzling and the sun shone in a cloudless blue sky. He stood beside the ship's rail and gazed at the sea; he could just make out a school of dolphins leaping in the distance, their bodies arching above the waves like a *corps de ballet*.

'Has His Majesty's Envoy slept well?'

Guillaume turned to the captain.

'I slept, Captain. Your medicine helped. Are we stationary?'

'Long enough for a catch of fish. Cook spied a group of swordfish, so the men are trying to harpoon them from the forecastle.'

Guillaume nodded.

'I should like to swim,' he said. 'Is it possible to go down into the water and swim?'

'Does His Majesty's Envoy know how to swim?' asked the captain in astonishment.

'Yes, a friend taught me on Isle de France.'

'I never thought a man of science, even an astronomer—'

'Would know how to swim?' Guillaume finished his sentence. 'Well, it happens that I do.'

'Are you quite certain?'

'That I should like to go for a swim?'

'No, sir, that you are capable of keeping afloat!'

Guillaume nodded.

'I'll order you a rope. Rope overboard!' The captain hollered the order, and the ship's boy scurried down to the hold.

Guillaume folded his clothes on the deck, but kept on his white cotton underpants, which came halfway down his thighs, fastened at the ends with silken bows. He lifted one leg then the other over the rail and prepared to descend the knotted rope, to the water. Several men of the crew, and the ship's boy, watched attentively. The sea was calm and smooth as oil. Guillaume let go of the final knot and took his first stroke out into the blue water. The vast, liquid expanse of azure enveloped his body, and he floated gracefully on the few wavelets breaking around the ship's hull. The captain stood with his men, watching Guillaume with folded arms.

'Is everything all right, Master Astronomer?' he called out.

Guillaume noted that his unexpected dip in the ocean, watched by the crew of the *Sylphide*, had promptly restored to him his old title from the *Berryer*.

'Everything is perfect, gentlemen!' he called back. And he wondered if they were not all equally astonished that a Master of the Académie des Sciences should know how to swim, when they themselves did not. Guillaume swam a few more strokes with a confidence that surprised even him. He was about fifty yards from the ship now. The experience was precisely what he needed, the morning after his sorry defeat. He looked up at the sun and he saw again the fleeting image of the tiny black marble passing in front of it. This great voyage for the merest glimpse of one of the most astonishing and rare phenomena known to astronomy: just a few, brief moments before it slipped from his sights. He plunged his head into the water, then slowly lifted it once more. Water, the source of life. Water everywhere, as far as the eye could see, all around him. As if all the continents of Earth had been submerged overnight, like Atlantis. Maps were of no interest, quite useless now, on a planet with no coastlines, no countries, no land. Just one ship, and the sun, and Venus passing by in another eight years, and a man afloat in the middle of the Indian Ocean. Himself. Guillaume Le Gentil de La Galaisière. For an ex-seminarian such as he, water meant contact with God, more powerful even than a line of music by Bach. It was water that John the Baptist poured over the face of Christ, water in the church fonts. Guillaume thought of the early Christian symbol for Christ: a fish. Something indefinable yet strangely coherent took shape in his mind. It was hard to formulate, like a word on the tip of your tongue that refuses to step into the light of conscious thought. This swim was more than a dip in the sea. It was a moment of communion with the beauty of the world, because his surroundings were beauty itself: the azure sky would turn black this night and fill with the stars of the Milky Way. The sun would set and the moon would rise, and tomorrow would be another day, and the next day, and the day after that. As it had been since the dawn of time, a distance no one could measure. 'Time,' said Guillaume quietly, as he swam smoothly, further from the ship. 'Life,' he added, with another breaststroke. 'Here I am in the midst of time and life. The midst of the universe. Afloat.'

The dolphins had swum nearer to this strange creature, all arms and legs, and soon he was surrounded by the great, pale grey fish, each pointing its smiling grey snout in his direction. The men on the ship were hollering words he could not hear. He saw the captain extending what looked like an eyeglass. Guillaume smiled at one of the dolphins. The creature fixed him with its small, laughing eye and opened its beak-like mouth, lined with tiny teeth. It gave a strange, high-pitched squeak. The others circled around him as if they had found a new playmate. The dolphin dived underwater and Guillaume felt himself lifted irresistibly, but with great care, by an astonishing force. Suddenly, he was no longer down in the water, but lying astride the dolphin's back, with nothing to cling to but its dorsal fin. The dolphin gave its high-pitched cackle of laughter and swam fast, followed by all the others, as if delighted by the joke it was playing on the swimmer.

On the deck of the *Sylphide*, the men of the crew stared in amazement. His Majesty's Envoy was riding on the back of a dolphin and racing towards them as fast as a hound on the heels of a fox. Guillaume held tight to the fin. The wind whipped his face, and he felt the speed with which these creatures moved through the waves. And it was then, riding the dolphin, in the Indian Ocean, that he understood what he must do, right then, at that moment of his existence. The decision came to him, as clear as the water through which he was moving. Yes, that was it. Of course. Everything made perfect sense. Even Hortense would approve. The dolphin slowed, and once again, Guillaume felt his legs and then his whole body enter the water. The four dolphins placed themselves in front of him and opened their beaks as if to hear what he had to say.

'My friends,' he told them. 'I have understood the path I must take. My path through life, the path that God has shown me, guided by the stars.' The dolphins nodded, in a chorus of cries.

'I'll tell you, hear what I say: I'm staying! I shall wait here, in the Indian Ocean, until the next transit of Venus in eight years' time! I won't go back to France. I have a rendezvous in eight years' time! I shall wait, and I shall be there!'

The four dolphins dived deep below the surface, then raced back up in single file, bursting out one after the other, nose first, soaring fully thirty feet into the air. Guillaume watched them, fascinated. Four great masses, a quarter of a ton apiece, spinning through the air as if weightless, and supple as cats. The dolphins each performed a nimble pirouette then dived straight down, nose-first, into their own element, sending four great sheaves of water into the air all around Guillaume.

'Yes! I'm staying!' he cried out, smacking the surface of the water with his hands. 'My mind is made up,' he said, as he climbed the last knots of the rope and stood trickling with seawater on the deck. 'I shall wait here for the next transit of Venus, in eight years' time.'

The chime of a text message sounded while Xavier was sleeping deeply, sailing through a strange dream in which two foxes were escorting him through a forest towards a naked woman who moved away in slow motion as he approached. He turned over in bed, looking incredulously at the time shown on his quartz alarm clock: 4:15 a.m. Who could it be at this hour? At first he didn't move, and then suddenly he started, thinking perhaps Céline had a problem with Olivier, that it was serious, that they were in hospital, in an ambulance, or God knows where. He felt around, cursing his glasses, without which he was incapable of reading the screen on his phone. He turned on his bedside lamp, blinked and unlocked the screen that was dazzling him with the message from Bruno.

CHARLOTTE IS SLEEPING WITH THE GARDENER!

It took Xavier a few seconds to digest this information, then to return to earth from the anxiety that had gripped him. Nothing that concerned him, then, nor his ex-wife, nor his son. Bruno, his friend, his ex-colleague at the agency, was clearly in a bad situation in the Dordogne, despite the tranquillity of The Dovecot. This was apparent from the fact that he had written to him in the middle of the night, when it had been months since they had properly spoken, not including their kind words of encouragement via Instagram. Xavier picked up the bottle of water next to his bed and lay back on the pillows.

SHALL I CALL YOU? he typed.

YES, Bruno replied. Xavier sipped some water, took a breath and pressed the call button. After one ring, Bruno answered.

'Charlotte is sleeping with the gardener,' was the first thing Bruno said, in a tone that was both gloomy and enraged.

'Yes,' Xavier replied. 'You just sent me that message, I read it, but really, Bruno, are you sure about this or is it just a suspicion?'

'She just admitted it!' Bruno shouted.

Xavier tried to maintain an impassive tone of voice which might, he thought, reassure his friend. 'Yes, well, then you're sure.'

'Yes, I'm sure, as you say,' Bruno replied sardonically, in a voice which brought to mind the jerky tone employed by Jack Nicholson in *The Shining*. 'And it's me who pays that gardener, pays him to plant the trees and trim the hedges, not to shag my wife!' he exploded.

Xavier didn't know what to say. He tried, 'You're right, that's not spelled out in his contract, I suppose.'

'No, not exactly,' Bruno said. There was a long silence.

'What does he look like, this gardener?' Xavier asked cautiously.

'Like a young Depardieu!' Bruno erupted. 'He's his twin, his clone! He looks just like Depardieu in *The Last Metro*, except instead of riding the metro, he's—'

'Have you been drinking, Bruno?' Xavier asked.

'Not a drop,' the other replied sharply. 'But maybe I will. I left the house to shut myself up in the barn and sleep in the hay. There's a bottle of brandy on the shelf that I don't think anyone has opened since the day Charles de Gaulle left for London.'

Xavier didn't know how to respond, and the late hour combined with the unexpected wake-up call wasn't helping his concentration. 'What did Charlotte say to you?' he asked, shifting on the pillows again.

'That she's been sleeping with him for three months. That's what she said.'

'But… how did she justify it?'

There was a laugh from the other end of the phone, then Bruno told him that one stormy afternoon he had gone to Ikea to look for furniture for one of the new bed and breakfast rooms – Dovecot No. 4. Charlotte had gone out to the vegetable patch that the gardener was fixing up for them, and it was there that the two of them had sheltered from the violent storm while Bruno was stuck with his Ikea boxes at a motorway tollbooth in a power cut. The young Gérard Depardieu lookalike had wrapped Charlotte in his coat so she didn't get soaked by the rain, then lit a fire in the hut by the vegetable patch. There, they had looked at each other, waiting for someone to make the first move.

'While I was stuck at the tollbooth, they were writhing around in front of the fire.' Bruno croaked.

'Do your daughters know?'

'No,' Bruno replied. 'She hasn't said anything since we argued, and I left to go and sleep in the barn – ostensibly to try out the new eco guest house where you sleep on hay and eat a rustic breakfast of country ham and eggs from our own hens.'

Xavier attempted one last question. 'Does Charlotte regret it?'

There was a long silence. 'No, she doesn't regret it, Xavier. She said she couldn't resist. Can you believe that? She couldn't resist.'

'It's like in *Lady Chatterley's Lover*,' Xavier said without thinking, before immediately regretting mentioning the book.

'Thanks for the literary reference, Xavier, that's very helpful,' said Bruno.

'Sorry,' said Xavier.

'It's okay,' said Bruno, then gave a long sigh. 'Now I've updated you on my colourful life in the country, what's going on with you?'

Xavier cleared his throat. 'Me?' he said. 'I'm… spending every day watching a woman who lives three streets away through an eighteenth-century telescope, and I think I'm falling in love with her. I was dreaming about her when you messaged me.'

There was another silence.

'Okay, don't move. I'm going to open the brandy.'

Xavier heard the sound of the phone being put down on some

furniture and then a stopper being pulled out.

Bruno picked up the phone and gave a boozy sigh. 'That's better!' he cried.

'Are you drinking from the bottle?' asked Xavier.

'Of course. I didn't have time to get a glass from the kitchen, did I? So, to sum up: I've had my wife stolen by the local gardener after twenty years of marriage and two children; and you are watching a woman through your window with a telescope, and you're mad about her. Xavier, I seem to recall we were once well-adjusted, intelligent men, who got our degrees and whose lives should have been a bit more ordinary. Right?'

'Yes, we were, and we still should be,' Xavier objected. 'But I haven't just been watching her. I've met her, ' he added.

'Oh yeah?!' Bruno exclaimed. 'How did it go? Did you get on well?'

'Yes, it went pretty well,' Xavier said tentatively. 'I think I'm going to offer her my apartment in exchange for hers.'

There was a silence.

'Okay, I get it, the world is nuts. I'm going to finish this bottle. I'll call you back. Goodnight.' Bruno hung up.

Xavier remained immobile in bed. Tonight, he had been of absolutely no help to his friend. He closed his eyes, only to open them again at the sound of another text message:

I TOLD BRUNO I WAS SLEEPING WITH THE GARDENER IN THE HEAT OF THE MOMENT BECAUSE HE WAS DRIVING ME CRAZY WITH ALL HIS SUSPICIOUS QUESTIONS OVER THE LAST TWO WEEKS. YOUR IDIOT FRIEND, WHO PRESUMABLY JUST CALLED YOU, BELIEVED ME AND NOW HE WON'T DROP IT!

Charlotte.

Xavier sighed. What could he do to change the outcome of this quarrel, worthy of a TV sitcom but playing out in real life, in the depths of the Dordogne? It was late, or early, depending on how you read the hands of a watch at this hour. He gave up on replying to her and reached to the floor for his copy of *Journey through the Seas of India*.

The small cemetery stood on the side of a hill. Guillaume pushed the wrought-iron gate, which creaked as it opened. The drystone walls were covered in ivy, and a riot of vegetation had taken root around the neglected graves, their headstones broken by the rain and wind. He saw the newest grave straightaway and drew closer to the freshly dug earth with its wooden cross, chiselled with a single word. A name: Toussaint. Guillaume stood in respect, took a deep breath, then went down on one knee and closed his eyes to pray. On his return to Isle de France, in the governor's guest house, after the maritime misadventures that had cost him the accurate observation of the transit of Venus, he had declared: 'I shall see my friend Toussaint, whom I never thought to see again!'

The remark had drawn silence from the French governor's domestic staff. 'You won't see him again, sir,' came the reply, and Guillaume had stopped dead, before turning slowly to face them.

'You're the astronomer,' said a female voice, and Guillaume looked in the direction of the cemetery gate. A woman, her skin as brown as Toussaint's, stood looking at him. She held a bouquet of ten freshly cut anthuriums in her right hand, their heads pointing down towards the ground. She walked towards him, and Guillaume got to his feet.

'I am indeed,' he said.

The woman nodded and gazed at the freshly dug earth covering the grave.

'You're the first Frenchman to pay his respects at my husband's resting place.' Then she looked up, into his eyes.

'Dear Guillaume, you're a good man,' she said, placing her hand on the astronomer's arm.

'Toussaint, too, was a very good man,' he said.

'Yes, he was,' she replied, turning her head to hide her tears, before adding, 'You'll meet again in the gardens of Paradise… you and the dodos.'

'He told you about the dodos?' said Guillaume quietly.

She nodded. And Guillaume put his arms around her as she fought to contain her sobs.

Toussaint's comrades explained to Guillaume that he had injured himself with a sickle while overseeing the cutting of a sugar cane plantation on the island. The wound had become infected, and then the fever had come. On the eighth day, exhausted, Toussaint had closed his eyes. An enamel-blue butterfly alighted on the top of the cross, closed its wings and seemed to be watching them closely.

'Tell me your first name?' asked Guillaume, as he loosened his embrace. They had addressed one another informally straightaway, not once pausing to reflect on the appropriateness or otherwise of such a thing.

'Aimée,' said the woman, wiping her eyes.

'Did you have children together?'

'Two,' she answered. 'Please, bless my flowers.' She held out the bouquet of anthuriums.

'Alas, I am not a priest,' said Guillaume sadly.

'You almost were,' she reminded him. 'Toussaint called you the "Priest of the Stars".'

Guillaume said nothing, then raised his hand and made the sign of the cross over the striking red flowers with their white, waxy pistils.

'In the name of the Father, the Son and the Holy Spirit, bless these flowers for the heart of a man who has entered Thy Kingdom. Amen.'

Aimée laid the flowers on the grave. They stood side by side for a long moment in silence. The butterfly was motionless, as if frozen.

'What are you doing here on the island?' Aimée wanted to know.

'I failed in my observation of the transit of Venus across the sun, and so I am going to wait eight years for the next occurrence. I shall map your island, and Isle de Bourbon and Madagascar. I shall note all my astronomical observations, the winds and the ocean currents. In eight years' time, if Pondicherry is inaccessible, perhaps I will sail to Manila – a good place from which to observe the transit.'

'Eight years is a long time, sailing from one island to the next across the seas of India,' said Aimée.

'Yes, a long time indeed,' Guillaume agreed.

'But then again, an eight-year wait is nothing,' she reassured him. 'I shall be spending the rest of my life here.' She fell silent, then smiled: 'You are devoted to your star, to Venus.'

'Yes, I believe I am. And I cannot truly say why.'

'What will you live on, for these eight years?'

'I have a little money of my own. And a benefactor, the Duc de La Vrillière, who may help me. My needs are few.'

'You don't have a wife?'

'I do,' said Guillaume quietly. 'She is waiting for me. That's what the keeper of the dodos told me.'

Aimée smiled. 'I must go.'

'Where do you live? If I should wish to see you again…'

'I live in the house with the red roof, behind the big green tree.' Aimée pointed to the far end of the cemetery. 'Toussaint told me that with your machine, you could see the moon as clearly as if you were walking on its surface.'

Guillaume smiled. 'You can come and see, one evening.'

She shook her head. 'I'm not allowed to visit the governor's guest house. Toussaint could, because he had been chosen, but not me.'

Guillaume thought for a moment, then sighed. 'Well, then one day I'll come to you, I'll come to see you and the children, with my telescope, and together we will walk on the moon.'

Aimée nodded.

'Good day, Guillaume.'

'Good day, Aimée.'

He stood for a moment at the graveside. The blue butterfly still had not moved. It rose up into the air just as Guillaume pulled the wrought-iron gate closed behind him.

That evening, alone in his quarters out on the balcony, Guillaume took out a knife. With its point, he marked a cross on his telescope.

'One cross, for one year in the seas of India.'

On just such another evening, with many more nights passed, there would be eight crosses on the gleaming copper tube.

'This is the dodo,' explained Alice. 'He's almost finished.'

Olivier approached the huge bird, almost a metre tall, perched on a wooden box. An immobile bird straight from a fairy tale, whose small yellow glass eyes were fixed on him.

'They disappeared at the end of the seventeenth century, or at the beginning of the eighteenth. A long time ago. So, we're restoring him from remains.'

Olivier moved slowly around the bird, touching its feathers with his fingertip. Alice turned towards Xavier, who smiled at her. Esther, Alice's daughter, stood before the bird, arms crossed, following Olivier carefully with her eyes.

Father and son had presented themselves at the museum entrance that Alice had indicated – not the main entrance that visitors came to, hoping to buy their tickets to the Grand Evolution Gallery, but rather a heavy door with an unmarked intercom. Xavier had rung the bell and a male voice had replied. He told him he had come to visit Alice Capitaine, and the voice replied: 'Come in.'

The door opened with a tinkling of bells. Xavier and Olivier found themselves in a courtyard filled with piles of rusty metal frames. You could make out the shapes of animals – a warthog, a big cat and some birds – which could just as easily have been displayed on pedestals in one of those sterile rooms beloved of contemporary art galleries for an 'installation'. All it needed was a title – *Animalia 3*, for instance.

An artist could have given a long, pompous speech about the concept, blending the ethereal shapes of the animals, the rust and the dangers threatening our planet. In the inner courtyard, a door opened and a man with a ponytail came to meet them.

'Are you Xavier and Olivier? My name is Pierre. Alice is in the workshop. Follow me.'

The three of them walked through the numerous corridors filled with shelves, which held shells, jars of reptiles suspended in formaldehyde, framed insects and stuffed birds, some of which had been deplumed.

'These have all come from reserves,' said Pierre. 'We've spent years trying to sort them out, but it's never-ending.'

Olivier's eyes roamed over the shelves filled with curiosities which stretched up to the ceiling. Everything was dusty and half-lit, and seemed as though it hadn't been moved for aeons.

'I'll show you something really curious,' Pierre said to Olivier. He paused to climb a small librarian's ladder on wheels and took down a jar of formaldehyde. 'You aren't scared of snakes, are you?' he asked. Olivier shook his head. 'Look. This was hunted in Napoleon's time, in 1812.'

Olivier and Xavier bent over to see a snake that looked like a viper.

'But…' said Olivier, 'it has three heads!'

'Yes,' Pierre replied. 'That's why we kept it. You don't see that every day, do you?' he added, replacing the jar on the shelf. 'We need to find him a good spot in the museum, but we have no room,' he lamented.

They began to walk once more through a maze of corridors. Old scientific posters about flora and fauna brightened up some of the walls, while on others, the paint was peeling. Finally, they arrived at a reinforced door, and Pierre typed in a code. The door opened with a click.

'Welcome to the workshop,' said the taxidermist. The room was enormous and entirely painted white. The lights were bright. Here, there was no peeling paint on the walls, no dusty jars. The desks in the workshop were scattered around, and before each one was a taxidermist at work, some standing, some sitting. A paintbrush in hand or their eyes behind an enormous magnifying glass, they oversaw their meticulous work in reverent silence. Some tables held just one animal, while others held several. The majority were covered in pins, and the workbenches were piled high with vials, bottles, tools, pliers, stamps, stylets… Olivier looked around, fascinated at this secret place where new, motionless life was given to the most beautiful and rare animals on the planet. He approached a man who seemed perplexed, examining an enormous black bat. He had placed it on a pedestal and was altering its small snout with the tip of his pliers. He must have been using a colourless varnish, because once the pliers had passed over it, the muzzle seemed suddenly moist and alive. On the other side of the room, Alice waved them over, and they headed towards her.

Wearing a white lab coat, she was sitting on a black leather chair with wheels and was moving around a giant bird placed on a box: a dodo. Seated next to her was a young girl of about ten years old, who stood up at Xavier and Olivier's approach. She had long brown hair, pale skin and the same dark eyes as her mother. Alice was about to speak when her daughter jumped in.

'I'm Esther,' she said, looking at Olivier. 'Welcome to the museum. We're making a dodo.'

Olivier nodded.

'I'm Olivier,' he began, 'and…'

'And I'm Xavier, Olivier's father,' said Xavier. 'Hello Esther, and hello Alice,' he said, turning towards the taxidermist.

'Hello Xavier,' said Alice with a smile. 'You two aren't frightened by our workshop?'

'Oh no,' cried Olivier. 'It's brilliant!' He approached the huge bird, stopping before its yellow gaze, then walking slowly around to its back and placing a finger on its feathers.

'I love Bernard's bat,' said Esther.

'Yes, I saw it,' Olivier replied.

'Let's go look again, he's almost finished.' Esther pulled Olivier over to the table with the bat. The taxidermist named Bernard looked at them and said, 'So, what do you think?'

Xavier smiled at Alice. 'Thank you,' he said. 'I think, thanks to you, my son is going to have an afternoon he won't soon forget.'

'He's not afraid, which is good,' Alice replied. 'A few months ago, Esther brought one of her friends and he was traumatised, and they haven't seen each other since. I think she had a little crush on him, too,' she added, with a small smile. She got up from her chair and pushed it away with the toe of her boot. 'Do you like it? I've been working on this bird for months. I dream about it at night.'

'The dodo... the extinct bird,' Xavier said softly 'It's amazing. It looks alive.'

'Then I've done my job,' said Alice. 'But it's not finished. I still need to put some colour on the feathers and put some make-up on the beak and around the eyes.'

'You put make-up on them?'

'Yes, always. It's the last step. It's what Bernard is doing with the bat, which is a real vampire bat. It's a giant bat from South America, one that attacks cattle.'

Xavier looked at Alice. Dressed in black beneath her lab coat like last time, she seemed so feminine and so unusual standing next to a bird that had been extinct since before the Revolution. He wanted to tell her how pretty she looked, but he didn't dare, saying instead: 'Where do all these animals come from?'

'From nature reserves,' Alice replied. 'None of them are a product of hunting, they all died a natural death, young or old. They notify us, or otherwise we submit a request for a specimen and one day they send it to us. It's all very strictly regulated by the Washington Convention.'

At the mere mention of the name, Xavier remembered that Alice might be living the next part of her life in the American capital.

'Would you like a coffee? I think our kids are well occupied,' she said, glancing over at Esther and Olivier, who were sitting side by side in two chairs while Bernard brought them an eagle with outstretched wings, perched on a stand.

Alice and Xavier drank their paper cups of coffee in silence.

'You have a very unique profession,' he said.

'And a very old one,' said Alice.

'Is it a calling?'

'Yes, in a way. My uncle was a salesman at Deyrolle, the famous taxidermy shop on Rue du Bac. I spent whole afternoons there when I was young. I had my favourite animals: the lion, the tiger, the pink budgie and the kiwi; I gave them names, stories, spoke to them,' she reminisced.

'Like Esther must speak to her flying fish.'

Alice smiled. 'Yes, she does – I can hear her through the wall. Let's show the kids the warehouse with the big animals,' she said, pointing to the children. 'Esther, Olivier, come this way!' The two jumped out of their chairs and thanked Bernard before joining them. Alice picked up a bunch of keys and unlocked a door. They then went through a security door across a courtyard to find themselves in a hangar made of steel beams like those on the Eiffel Tower, with an enormous tiled roof. Alice entered a code and the large double-panelled doors opened with an electronic hiss. The neon lights illuminated one after the other, flickering as they stabilised, and Olivier was dumbstruck. Animals stood on either side of the huge bay as far as the eye could see. There were five giraffes, four elephants, a rhinoceros, lions, tigers and gorillas. A shark hung in the air, alongside a small sperm whale; a camel and a dromedary stood side by side, as though they were awaiting their Bedouin, while a polar bear on its hind legs seemed to search for the arrival of the coming aurora borealis. The motionless scene was perfectly unreal, and Olivier followed Esther as she introduced the animals one by one, accustomed as she was to the place – delighted to feel that what seemed exceptional to others had become quotidian to her.

'It's fascinating,' said Xavier, as the children sped off without paying them any attention. 'It's Noah's Ark.'

Alice nodded.

'Well said. That's what we call it here. It's a real treasure. There are hardly any collections of this size in the world.' They walked slowly through the bay. For a moment it seemed to Xavier that they were in the nave of a cathedral, that they were walking together to the altar for their marriage under the eyes of a congregation consisting entirely of outsized animals.

'I'm happy your son is having fun here. You're divorced, if I've understood correctly?'

'Yes,' Xavier agreed. 'It's not always easy.'

Alice nodded.

'And you?' he asked.

'No,' Alice replied. 'I'm raising my daughter alone because she never knew her father. He died before she was born. A diving accident in Corsica. I loved diving too,' she added, 'but that summer I couldn't go under. I was six months pregnant, so I waited on the beach. And he didn't come back up alive. I've never gone diving since,' she said quietly.

'I'm sorry,' Xavier said gently.

'I think the kids have shaken us off. Esther!' Alice called, and the girl appeared behind a bison, followed by Olivier. 'I'm showing him Archibald!' Esther cried, before disappearing once more.

'Archibald is her name for the vulture,' Alice clarified.

'And your zebra?'

'He's gone to his owner's home. I think he's doing well. The owner invited me to come and visit him one evening over drinks.'

There was a silence between them, and Xavier caught the eye of a caribou who seemed to be encouraging him make the leap.

'I'd like to show you another apartment,' he said. 'I think it fits what you're looking for: balcony, separate kitchen, two bedrooms, a big living room. It's in the neighbourhood, close to your house.'

He was very close to home. On a beach near Coutances. His black boots sank into the sand as he climbed the dune dotted with tufts of grass and dry seaweed carried ashore by the wind. At the very top of the small rise, he found Toussaint, sitting in the sand in front of a fire. His friend from Isle de France was surrounded by stacks of papers, which he placed one by one on the glowing logs, each catching fire as he did so. Guillaume approached and recognised his own handwriting, his correspondence with Hortense. Toussaint looked up at him and smiled. Guillaume greeted him with a nod. Then Toussaint pointed to a bowl of steaming milk that stood as if waiting for him, on a tree stump. Guillaume took the bowl and lifted it to his lips. Immediately, he recognised an aroma and a taste from far, far away. Milk with carrageen, a red algae properly known as *Chondrus crispus*, a recipe handed down the ages but now almost forgotten. The seaweed was steeped in warm milk, then removed, and the thick, salty, almost pearly mixture drunk for its many medicinal benefits. His grandmother had made it for him as a child, and he had never drunk a bowl of milk like it since. Guillaume turned to look at the sea, and saw that it was blue and calm, a thing unknown in these parts. It looked more like the Indian Ocean. The bowl disappeared from his right hand and now he was standing on the beach. Squinting in the bright sunlight, he saw the silhouette of a little girl walking towards him. She was barely ten years old, and Guillaume recognised the youngest daughter of his parents' friends, the Potiers. The girl approached him and smiled. It was indeed Marie-Michelle Potier. Whenever he visited her parents' house, on the few occasions when he returned from Paris to spend time with his family in Normandy, she would run to greet him, hurling herself at his legs or flinging her arms around his waist and calling out his name, 'Guillaume! Guillaume!' Several times, he had shown her the stars through a telescope, and even without a telescope on one dark summer's night, telling her each of their names. Ever since then, before going to sleep, she would say her prayers and count off the names of the stars like a poem. The last time he saw her, just before he boarded the *Berryer*, he had gone home to bid farewell to his family and friends. Marie-Michelle had clutched him tight.

'Don't go, Guillaume!' she had begged, stifling a sob.

Guillaume had knelt down, level with her gaze, and wiped a tear from her cheek with his finger.

'I'll be back,' he whispered in her ear, 'and I'll have so many stories to tell you.'

Marie-Michelle slipped her small hand into his and they walked together, towards the sea. Dolphins were jumping in the distance, and Guillaume looked up to see planets in the sky, close overhead: Venus, Jupiter, even Saturn with its rings. They reached the first wavelets, and their feet did not sink, but stayed on the surface. Guillaume's black leather boots and Marie-Michelle's little laced slippers trod the surface, and they walked on the water as if it were the blue, tanned hide of an animal. They walked on the water, and the planets were closer still.

Guillaume opened his eyes. A plain white ceiling supplanted the vision of Saturn and its rings. He was back in his quarters on Isle de France. He stared at his right hand, which seconds before had held Marie-Michelle's. It was empty. He sat up, lifted the mosquito net and walked across to the balcony. The sky was black as ink and scattered with stars in the warm night. He was leaning on the balcony railing with his eyes closed, when he was startled by a flutter of wings. A black bird with a golden yellow beak had alighted at arm's length. The creature fixed him with its beady eye, then opened its beak: 'The transit of Venus!' it squawked, in raucous tones. And again, 'The transit of Venus!' as if alarmed by its own pronouncement.

'Molière?' said Guillaume quietly, moving closer.

'Master Astronomer!' A man's voice called from the darkness of the garden below, and Guillaume made out a silhouette.

'Captain Vauquois?'

'The very same!' came the voice. 'Forgive me for calling at this late hour, but I was determined to try my luck. I was told earlier this evening that you were here. The *Berryer* sails at dawn, and I felt I must see you!'

'Come up, Captain!'

A few moments later, he opened his door to Louis de Vauquois, who greeted him with a broad smile. The captain's myna bird flew across the room to land on his shoulder.

'Come in, Captain, I'm delighted to see you again!' said Guillaume. 'There's a decent French wine left on the table – we can share a couple of glasses.'

They sat and drank.

'What are you still doing here on Isle de France, Master Astronomer?'

'A long story,' sighed Guillaume, 'and I fear it will be much longer still,' he added with a smile.

The captain looked him in the eye.

'The crew of the *Berryer* send their greetings, and I shall drink to your guiding star, sir.' Together they raised a toast, and their glasses rang softly in the night.

'The terrace,' said Xavier, as he opened the sliding glass door and Alice walked into the sunlight. For the last twenty minutes he had been showing her his apartment, which he had scrupulously tidied, cleaning the rug with the Dyson, the kitchen with white vinegar, and the tiles with a window-cleaning product. Whether or not to tell Alice that this was his apartment had been the morning's dilemma. Faced with the impossibility of deciding if this confession was wise, he had resorted to flipping a twenty-cent coin, catching it and turning it over on his hand. 'Tails, I tell her it's my house, heads, I do nothing.' The coin had shown an image of the Umberto Boccioni sculpture of the man in movement. Heads.

Alice had met him at the agency to view the apartment which, according to him, had many of the features she had been looking for.

'I didn't see it in your window,' she noted.

'No, we haven't done a photo session with Monsieur Chamois yet; it just came on the market.' When Xavier announced the address of the place they were going to visit, Chamois had looked up from his computer and fixed his eyes on him. That morning, even the voice – which was still a male voice – had encouraged Xavier to take a step back from things and let go of the reins of life, over which he had no control. Xavier had felt the weight of his feet and concentrated on his breathing. He noticed that his heart rate sped up a little when he thought of Alice. *Put external thoughts from your mind, gently but firmly*, the voice had advised.

His heart rate sped up even more when he turned the key in his own lock to allow Alice to enter first. He had done a last sweep of the apartment and removed the photo frame where he featured several times with Olivier in a collage of digital photos from over the years. The entrance, the bedroom, the second bedroom, and the kitchen, separated from the rest of the apartment, had pleased Alice greatly. Now the balcony terrace, the apartment's greatest asset, might turn her hesitation into a 'Yes, I'm very interested', which would open up a field of previously unimagined possibilities for Xavier: sell her his own apartment and buy hers with the money. It was completely mad and would need some explanation, but at that precise moment, and in spite of his pounding heart, he felt extraordinarily light. Finally, something interesting and unexpected was happening in his life. Although he wasn't entirely the engineer of this thing, he could be said to be its silent accomplice.

'The view is stunning. It's the same one I have from my top room, but much less obstructed,' Alice called, before turning towards the shutters and the telescope, which Xavier had pushed against them.

'There's a telescope,' she said.

Xavier contented himself with saying: 'Yes.'

'It looks very old. Does it work, do you think?'

Xavier cleared his throat. 'I imagine so.'

'Let's try it,' said Alice. 'I'm sure I can see my windows from here.'

Xavier placed the telescope on its iron stand and moved it to the place it had occupied since he had taken it from the sold apartment. Alice leaned over the eyepiece and moved the tube's viewfinder until it fell on her apartment.

'Got it!' she exclaimed. 'You can see it really clearly.'

Xavier ran a hand through his hair. This time, he wondered what the meditation voice would tell him to do. Alice was on his terrace, looking into her apartment just as he did every day.

'Monsieur Sorbier is watering his plants,' she observed. 'He's my neighbour.' She straightened up and contemplated the telescope as it shone in the sunlight.

'There are eight crosses engraved here.' She ran a finger over the notches in the copper tube. Xavier followed her delicate hand, with its impeccably manicured nails, a hand which could also, with precise movements and needles, give a second, motionless life to animals.

'How much is this apartment?' she asked, turning towards him, and Xavier had the feeling of parachuting out of the open door of an aeroplane. Bruno had done such a jump – a baptism of air rather than fire. He had recorded a video which had frozen Xavier with fear. The video showed Bruno, his instructor behind him, floating in emptiness, in a brightly coloured flying suit and transparent skydiving goggles. Bruno smiled throughout the whole video, shrieking with joy. Unlike his friend and colleague, Xavier was not suspended in mid-air at 180 miles an hour, but rather was standing on his terrace before Alice Capitaine.

'How much?' he repeated. 'I'll have to analyse a couple of factors, but it's basically the same price as yours. Even if they have different layouts, the surface area is the same and they are like for like on the market.' As soon as he said these words, Xavier immediately regretted his salesman's language, that civilised vocabulary of cold politeness. The only thing he wanted to say was, Alice, I think you're beautiful, charming and so unique, and I think I'm falling in love with you.

Alice wanted to look at the bedroom again, and the second bedroom, then the kitchen and the bathroom.

'You have room for another zebra,' Xavier pointed out as they returned to the living room, and Alice smiled.

'Did Olivier enjoy his visit to the museum?'

'Oh yes,' Xavier replied. 'He talks about it all the time.'

'While she waits for him to come back,' Alice said, rummaging through her handbag, 'Esther wanted to give Olivier a souvenir. She chose this,' she said, pulling out a small paper bag with ribbon handles. 'I won't tell you what it is; it'll be a surprise for your son.'

Xavier took the bag, which was feather-light. 'Thank you,' he said, touched. 'I'll give it to him this weekend. Give Esther a hug from both of us. I'll keep it safe,' he said, moving towards a shelf in the room, then stopping in his tracks. How could he keep a present safe in an apartment that wasn't his?

'I'll keep it with me and take it back to the agency,' he said firmly. The two of them looked at each other in silence for a moment, then Xavier spoke. 'I'd like to give you something too, but I don't have anything, unfortunately.'

Alice seemed to think for a moment, then turned her dark, liquid eyes on him.

'You can give me your presence.'

'Excuse me?' Xavier mumbled.

'Luigi Nessi,' she said. 'My Italian scholar, collector of zebras, has invited me for drinks at his house to show me the animal back in its setting. He's a gourmand who loves good wine, but… I don't want to go alone. Would you like to come with me?'

The wine paired beautifully with the warm, succulent, salty flesh, grilled on its top side and fragrant with aromatic herbs. Guillaume nibbled the delicious chunks of *Lobatus gigas*, straight from a pointed stick that served as a skewer. In this part of the Indian Ocean, the huge shellfish was better known as a *lambi*, or queen conch. They could measure up to a foot across, and their shell alone was one of the beauties of nature, with a rose-window pattern that spiralled to a cream-coloured, pointed tip. A row of porous, horn-shaped spikes ran around the spiral, and the porcelain body tapered like a cone of delicately folded parchment. When you turned the *lambi* over, the shell flared to reveal an unexpected, deep shade of pink, silky-smooth, with a sheen as bright as enamel.

Until now, such exotic seashells, like something out of a fairy tale, were known to Guillaume only as basins for holy water in the cathedrals of France, their crenellated edges invariably set with copper or brass, as bright as gold. They would stand on a tall base against the first pillars of the nave; the faithful would dip their fingers before crossing themselves. He had always found it hard to think of such giant shells as anything other than works of art – it seemed impossible that they should come from the bottom of the sea, where they lay among the rocks and coral, sheltering a mollusc the size of a small dog. The holy water basins, and the *lambis*, all came from beneath the Indian Ocean where, unbelievably, he had been living, surrounded by those blue waters, on an island at the ends of the Earth – he, Guillaume Le Gentil de La Galaisière – for two years already, and another six still to come.

The readings he had taken around Isle de France had been a source of great satisfaction – they differed significantly from the charts currently used by His Majesty's navy. Guillaume had also undertaken to map the Isle de Bourbon, a French possession of comparable size, close by to the south-west, and it was here, in his idle moments between observations of the stars, waiting for the next transit of Venus in front of the sun, that he had begun to assemble a precise, thoroughly scientific collection of seashells. The governor of Isle de France had given him an old encyclopaedia with an entire chapter on the shells of the seas of India. The work included engravings of hundreds of varieties, each one named and referenced. The few collections he had seen on his visits to the museum in Paris were nothing compared to what he could gather here in a single afternoon, strolling at the water's edge. To bring home for the institution a near-complete collection of specimens from this region seemed to him a worthy and absorbing scientific occupation, and one he could complete with success over these eight years. He decided to have the governor's staff make eight large wooden chests, big enough for two men to lie down inside. Each chest would contain seven rows of drawers divided into compartments of various sizes, from the very large to the minuscule, each capable of holding one or several shells, big or very small. The carpenters were delighted at the prospect – a welcome change from their usual rafters, floorboards and balustrades – and a blacksmith on the island undertook to forge the clasps and locks, complete with seven keys which he presented to Guillaume, swinging from a single steel ring. Each chest could hold between 800 and 1,000 seashells. The chests followed him everywhere now, like the empty luggage of some distinguished traveller of no fixed abode, and no real destination.

'This *lambi* is a great delicacy. I have eaten nothing so succulent since the giant lobsters on Isle de France,' said Guillaume, finishing his second stick. He was sitting on a beach in Madagascar, surrounded by Aldebert and five islanders, who had caught and prepared the meal they were all sharing on the white sand of the east coast, in this year of 1763. Aldebert was a thickset, bald man of indeterminate age. He had come from France and lived here now. No one knew how he made his living or even why he had come to Madagascar in the first place; only that he served the French Crown and welcomed travellers sent by the king's military governor. It was said he was an escaped convict, discreetly pardoned by His Majesty. He was rumoured to be a nobleman, or a peasant, or a sailor, or a soldier. It was even said that he was the son of the mysterious Man in the Iron Mask. No one knew who Aldebert truly was, but he was a trusted guide and host – in the words of the governor of Isle de France, who had written Guillaume a brief letter of introduction with a goose-quill pen on parchment, sealed in quivering hot red wax with a stamp of the ring he always wore.

Guillaume's plan for the coming year was to map the east coast of Madagascar, where he had established his new quarters. To observe the winds and currents, too, of course, and to continue his collection of seashells. On his first meeting with Aldebert, the fellow had appeared bare-chested, wearing only broad canvas pantaloons and a pair of brown leather boots. His chest and even his enormous belly were covered with a great variety of tattoos, among which the only motifs Guillaume could decipher were a lily and a crucifix. Draped around his shoulders, an animal like none the astronomer had ever seen before fixed him with orange eyes: the creature looked like a cross between a monkey and a cat, grey and white, with a very long, striped tail. 'It's a ring-tailed lemur. They thrive here,' Aldebert had told him, simply. 'I rescued it when it was very small, and since then it has accompanied me like a domestic cat, but with hands.' Aldebert lived alone in a large house facing the ocean, in which he had offered Guillaume an entire floor to set up his astronomical equipment and his seashell chests. He was a man of few words, but his silences were those of a man of discretion, rather than a bad or sullen character.

As the weeks went by, the big man had shown a growing attachment to Guillaume – their observation of a red comet one evening, through the telescope, had helped break the ice and established the astronomer as a true scientist in his eyes, capable of observing through his lenses things that no man on Earth could see with the naked eye. Truly, Guillaume was more than just another bothersome envoy of His Majesty, enlisting Aldebert's Malagasy men for days at a time to pick up empty shells from the beach and peer at them through a magnifying glass.

'I'm delighted it's to your taste, Le Gentil,' he said, as he enjoyed his own stick of *lambi*. A man signalled to him from a slender boat floating on the pale blue water as if suspended in air, and Aldebert shielded his eyes from the sun the better to see.

'Will you have some more?'

'Oh yes, with great pleasure,' said Guillaume. 'I have a favour to ask of you,' he added. 'I should like to open and cook the next *lambi* myself, if your men will show me how.'

Guillaume watched them carefully as they worked: first, make a hole in a precise spot near the top of the shell, using a hammer. Then insert the point of a knife to sever the mollusc's foot. Remove it from the shell with another, curved knife, cut away the inedible parts and peel off a sort of black skin to extract the iridescent white flesh.

'Granted!' Aldebert smiled.

He called out in Malagasy to the fisherman, who took a deep breath and dived into the water straightaway, in search of two more shellfish.

'You're a man who likes to understand everything,' Aldebert observed, filling their two glasses with wine. 'How the stars work, the sea, the sun, even how to open a *lambi*.'

'Indeed, I try to comprehend and make sense of the world,' said Guillaume quietly.

Aldebert nodded respectfully.

'Have you read Homer's *Odyssey*?' he said, after a moment's silence. 'It's the only great work I've read in my life. My voyage ends right here, I won't carry on to the end. But you, Le Gentil, you'll carry on, and one day you'll return home, like Odysseus.'

Guillaume was unsure how to respond. 'If you say so, Aldebert.'

The other man nodded, bit off another chunk of *lambi* and savoured it at length.

'Here, Le Gentil, time has no meaning. Time does not exist, it washes over me. I don't even know how old I am. Sometimes, I no longer know what year it is, do you understand?'

Guillaume gazed at the horizon. 'I think I understand,' he said. 'I've been here two years and sometimes it seems as if I landed last week. At other times, I feel I've been here for more than a century.'

'Yes, that's how it is,' Aldebert agreed. 'The enchantment of the Indian seas, and their curse.'

The diver returned to the surface holding a huge *lambi* in each hand.

'Excellent catch!' said Aldebert. He finished his stick and stood up.

'Come,' he said to Guillaume, and the two of them walked across to a great wooden plank that was placed directly on the sand. Next to the plank there was a wrought-iron grill, balanced on four large stones and glowing red-hot over the embers of the fire. Another group of four men were sitting around, eating the shellfish on long sticks. The fisherman emerged and came over to them, smiling and dripping seawater. His two shellfish weighed easily a few pounds each. Words were exchanged in Malagasy, a language Guillaume did not understand, but which Aldebert spoke fluently. The men laughed. Aldebert laughed too.

'They're making fun of me,' he explained, turning to Guillaume. 'They say I'm too fat to swim and fetch *lambi*, and I don't even know how to prepare one. They're right, I've never caught one. They say that a slim man like you, who knows how to swim and picks up seashells everywhere he goes, would have no difficulty at all.'

The *lambis* were placed side by side on the plank of wood. Guillaume and the fisherman knelt in front of them. The sea-swimmer delivered the first hammer-blows to the top of the shell, then showed Guillaume how to insert the knife. He took hold of the other knife and extracted the mollusc. Guillaume nodded, positioned the hammer himself between two spikes on the shell, and began to strike it. Aldebert and the other two men stood around in a circle. Guillaume made a hole in the shell and inserted the blade. He found the creature's foot, then used the other knife to pull it out.

'Excellent work,' said Aldebert, and the men all voiced their agreement. The fisherman took back the knife and separated the inedible parts, then split the mollusc in two. He handed the knife back to his neighbour, who had been watching him attentively. Guillaume cut the same parts from the second shellfish, but his blade struck something hard. Guillaume worked the knife around it, and the mollusc split in two. A silence fell, followed by low murmurs.

'Le Gentil…' breathed Aldebert. 'And your first *lambi*, too…'

A pearl of the same dark pink as the underside of the shell had appeared, nestled in the flesh. A perfectly round, iridescent pearl the size of a marble. The fisherman said something in his own language and Aldebert nodded before translating:

'These are the rarest pearls in the world. His grandfather found one. But he has never seen one before in his life.'

Guillaume closed his fingers around the pearl then lifted it out and held it up. A tiny, shimmering pink planet, its colours shifting in the light. He held it out to the fisherman, who gazed at it for a long moment, then nodded. The pearl was passed around from hand to hand, and finally to Aldebert, who inspected it and handed it back to Guillaume. A man said something, and Aldebert addressed him before turning to Guillaume.

'He says this is the ocean's gift to you, that you could sell it for a great deal of money, but that you should keep it for yourself.' The man added a few words, and Aldebert translated again: 'Or give it to the woman you love.'

Guillaume could not take his eyes off the perfect, pink sphere. He answered softly: 'Tell him I shall do as he says.'

Xavier returned to the apartment for a simple lunch of a tomato, some toast and olive oil, with a piece of cheese. He ate on the terrace, in the sun, as the weather had cleared since the morning. Chamois had left for lunch, too, and would open the agency when he returned. For the first time, a young woman had been waiting for Frédéric at the shop front; he had given her a discreet wave from his desk. She wore glasses and had a long blond plait. When Xavier looked at her, she averted her eyes. Chamois has a girlfriend, Xavier thought. If he happened to see the girl again on the pavement opposite, he would ask Chamois who she was – not out of idle curiosity, but to forge a connection with Chamois himself, who was not by nature a big talker. Xavier had thought too about what Bruno would have said: 'You've got yourself a new ladyfriend?' Chamois would have blushed. 'Who's that girl with the glasses across the street?' Bruno would have insisted. Poor Bruno. What was going on with his Depardieu-lookalike gardener? I must call him back, thought Xavier, slicing his tomato. He added a dash of olive oil and placed his warm toast on the plate along with two pieces of parmesan from the Italian grocer's. The prices kept going up; soon parmesan would be listed next to gold on the market. He went to sit on the terrace. The sun was so strong that he regretted leaving his sunglasses at the agency. The fresh basil leaves on the tomato were perfect, and the toast was just crunchy enough. Parmesan added a salty note to the dish. Everything was quiet, and Xavier stretched his hand towards Guillaume's telescope to lay his fingers on the shining copper. It couldn't be good for the instrument, leaving it in the full sun; he moved it back to its table, which was in the shade. His lunch finished, he poured himself a glass of iced Vichy water, then moved his chair closer to look through the lens of the telescope. The first thing he saw was Alice's window. He couldn't make anything out. She must have been at the museum, her daughter at school. The small bag she had left as a gift for Olivier from Esther was at the agency; he would give it to him this weekend. Since the viewing of his own apartment, Xavier really hadn't stopped thinking of Alice. Her face and her figure came to his mind at the most unexpected moments. And that feeling that something about her was familiar had not gone away – but what was it? He turned the telescope to the left, two buildings away from Alice's, and discovered a roof terrace which he had never noticed before, and which was occupied by a small team of professionals who were working with a fashion model. The young girl posed, half haughty, half sulky, while a crouching man held a large white reflective panel at her side. The photographer moved around the model, his eyes glued to the digital screen. Further away, a costume designer and her assistant seemed to be debating the next outfit. The photographer stopped his circling, then a make-up artist rushed towards the model and swept a brush over her face, while a young man brought her a paper cup of water. Xavier turned the telescope to the right, and the lens fell on a square window up high, on the fifth floor. A white sheet of what looked like printer paper was pressed to the windowpane from the inside. A sentence was written on it in black felt-tip pen. Xavier zoomed in to make out the text: PLEASE HELP ME, in English, that now international language, followed by a French mobile phone number. Xavier paused on the window for a few seconds to get his breath back. The piece of paper didn't move. He took out his biro from his jacket pocket and started to write down the phone number on his paper napkin from lunch. The moment he wrote down the last digit, the paper suddenly disappeared from the window, and Xavier stood dumbfounded. He looked again. Nothing there. No movement through the window. No shadows. Nothing.

PLEASE HELP ME.

He lowered the telescope and was motionless for a moment. A joke? A prank? One of those internet games spreading across the city?

Or not?

He poured himself another glass of sparkling water and looked at the numbers he had written down almost blindly with the biro on the napkin. The desire for a cigarette flashed across his mind, only to disappear just as quickly. What would the lost female voice say? Set your thoughts aside and concentrate on your breathing? He was breathing hard now, for sure. He was the involuntary witness to something that was clearly not right. He took out his phone from his pocket, and hesitated for a moment, before slowly dialling the number. Once he reached the last digit, he hesitated once more, before pressing the call button.

The first ring sounded, then the second, and then someone picked up.

'Hello,' said a man's voice, serious and cold.

'Hello,' Xavier replied, then there was a silence.

'Who's calling?' the serious voice asked.

Xavier wondered where to start. He took a deep breath, then said: 'I'm… on a balcony in Paris, and I just saw a piece of paper in the window opposite that had PLEASE HELP ME written on it, followed by your phone number.'

There was silence on the other end, then the man began to breathe deeply, as if he too was suddenly short of air. 'Where are you?' he asked sharply.

'At my house,' Xavier replied feebly, as a shiver went down his spine.

'What's going on, General?' he heard a new voice say.

'We've found number four,' the serious voice answered.

'Number four has been located!' the other voice cried, and it seemed to Xavier that a sudden excitement had erupted on the other end of the line.

'Who are you?' Xavier asked, swallowing his saliva with difficulty.

'I was going to ask you the same question,' the voice replied. 'But they've already brought me the answer. Do you believe in France, Monsieur Lemercier?'

'You know my name?'

'Yes,' the man replied. 'Your phone number is listed. Are you at home, Monsieur Lemercier?'

'Yes,' Xavier said quickly.

'I'll repeat my question. Do you believe in France?'

'Yes, I believe in France,' Xavier said.

'Well now you have a chance to prove it,' said the man, 'by helping us. I'm coming to you now. Don't move.'

'I'm not moving. There's a code for the building door and...'

But the man wasn't listening to Xavier. He had got up and walked away, surrounded by other men crying orders, and then the line went dead.

It had been less than twenty-five minutes – during which Xavier remained seated on the sofa trying to figure out what was going on – when he turned his head at the sound of the apartment buzzer. He stood up, went to the hallway, and opened the door to a man well into his fifties with short, chestnut-brown hair, wearing a grey uniform. Xavier craned his neck to see a dozen men behind the first.

'Monsieur Lemercier, I am General Delieue.' He shook his hand.

'Xavier Lemercier,' Xavier replied. 'Come in.'

The men flooded into the living room and immediately headed for the balcony, led by the general.

'We don't have much time,' he said to Xavier. 'Tell me everything, but very, very quickly.'

Xavier took a deep breath and pointed to the telescope.

'My telescope – it's a real museum piece which belonged to a famous astronomer. I thought I would use it to look at the stars with my son, or at the city when I am bored. It's pointed at the window in question, you can see.'

The general jerked his chin at one of the men, who went to look through the lens.

'It's Rue de la Mascarine,' he announced. Another man came up to him and took out a tablet with a detailed 3D plan of the neighbourhood, which Xavier recognised from Google Earth. 'It's number three, the fifth floor,' said the man. A third man, stouter than the others, came towards the general and said, 'The team is in the area.'

'Give them the position of the building,' the general said, and the man moved away. 'Monsieur Lemercier, we are going to install a very temporary command post in your apartment.'

One of the men took out the walkie-talkies and placed them on the table on the terrace; another plugged in a laptop by removing a lamp from its socket and covered his ears with a headset; while the others talked on their phones in low voices, pacing back and forth. Xavier watched them make themselves at home in his apartment as if they'd been there for years. He looked again at the military man, with his impassive face and his grey uniform.

'Are you the army? The secret service?'

The general inclined his head with a half-smile.

'Yes,' said Xavier. 'That was a stupid question.'

The general remained still, his gaze fixed on the floor of the building in question.

'I owe you an explanation,' he said eventually. 'Terrorism is one of the cancers of our time. One of our undercover agents has been exposed, and we lost all trace of him three weeks ago. You found him,' he said, turning to Xavier. 'Thank you.'

A walkie-talkie crackled on the table.

'RAID commander to General Delieue, over.'

'Delieue here, over,' replied the officer, picking up the walkie-talkie.

'The unit is now progressing up through the building, two men are heading for the roof, over,' said the voice.

'Copy that, over,' said Delieue. He pulled a liquorice stick from his pocket and wedged it between his teeth as though chewing on a cigarette. The man's calm was impressive, and Xavier didn't know what to do or say. He almost wanted to apologise for living there. One of the men handed the digital binoculars to the general. He held them up to his eyes, the liquorice stick making a quick rotation between his teeth.

'You can get behind the telescope, Monsieur Lemercier.'

Xavier sat on his chair and put his eye to the lens.

'I see your men,' said the general. 'I'm in position on the western axis, over.'

'Copy that,' said the voice. 'The operation will proceed upon your go-ahead, General, over.'

Through the lens of the telescope, Xavier saw the zinc roof of the building on which two men dressed in black with balaclavas and guns had just landed. They approached the chimney, testing the roof's sturdiness, then each took out a steel rope and wrapped it around the brick stack. They were communicating to each other by gesticulating with gloved hands and nodding. They attached themselves to the ropes using karabiners on their jumpsuits and backed up a few steps to stand on the edge of the roof. One of them raised his arm, holding out his thumb. Then they picked up their guns and were still. Xavier was holding his breath. He had time to throw a quick glance at the officer, still impassive, but chewing on the liquorice stick now. Everything seemed frozen.

'Go ahead,' said the general.

The two men jumped backwards into thin air. At the fifth floor, the rope swung and projected them, feet and guns first, towards the window. The windowpanes broke with a crash and their bodies went through. There were flashes from inside the apartment. Then nothing. The silence felt interminable to Xavier.

Then suddenly the walkie-talkie crackled. 'Operation complete. Target is alive. I repeat: the target was rescued alive. Target is in a bad way, but alive. The enemy attempted to kill the target at the moment of rescue… none of my men are hurt. Regrettably there are four dead, the four occupants of the apartment. Requesting a civil security helicopter Dragon EC145 to transport the injured target, over.'

'Thank you, men, good work, over,' said the general.

He chewed once more on his liquorice stick and then put it back in his pocket, before turning to Xavier, who stood up from his chair and asked: 'How many terrorist attacks do you prevent?'

'A lot, but we can't prevent them all,' the officer said with regret. 'You have performed a great service to me and to France, Monsieur Lemercier. If ever one day I can return the favour, you have my phone number.'

Xavier nodded. All the men stood up in the living room, the lamp was put back in its socket, and the walkie-talkies were stashed in suitcases.

'Let's go, men,' the general instructed them, and the man in front opened the apartment door. 'You may discuss what happened,' the general said to Xavier. 'But I would still prefer if you would keep it to yourself.'

'You can count on me, sir,' said Xavier. 'Even if I write my memoirs one day, I'll never tell anyone what I saw here.'

The officer nodded and followed the last man out of the apartment, before asking: 'What was the name of the famous astronomer the telescope belonged to?'

'Guillaume Le Gentil.'

Hortense,

My dearest beloved, I am writing at the height of the monsoon, and the wind is blowing hard. I must speak with the tip of my pen, and my ink – which, I should note, I have been making myself these past few weeks, by drying then emptying out the ink sacks of the octopuses I catch. The end product is a small black stone, very dry and hard, which I dissolve in a few drops of spring water. Five years now in the Indian seas, and seashells follow me everywhere, like a strange cortège, as I sail the blue ocean waves. I feel I know these coasts better even than the fish who swim below! I have seen several lunar eclipses and comets that no subject of His Majesty could hope to glimpse from France. I note down a thousand details about the peoples I encounter: their clothing, manners, beliefs. From an astronomer, I have become an explorer now, perhaps even an adventurer. I have no news from the Duc de La Vrillière, to whom I have written several times, and I am living on the *louis d'or* he sent me, though the supply will soon be exhausted. I dabble in business, too: there are precious hardwoods here which are of great value. I have two associates. We have launched some ventures together, of which the

Académie would doubtless disapprove, but a man has to live, albeit frugally, day to day. I eat nothing but fish, caught by my own or the islanders' hands. I find myself on an extraordinary journey, in which the elegant carriages of Paris seem like the shimmering mirages of a different civilisation altogether, perhaps even a dream. A remarkable man – Aldebert, about whom I have written before – has entertained me several times on my trips to Madagascar. He talks of how time flows differently in these balmy regions of the globe. He is quite right. Nothing here is the same as in France. The country people of my home region of Normandy, our fishermen, and the men of learning at the Académie des Sciences seem to me like luminous shades encountered in another life. You alone are my ever-shining Sun. News reaches me in scraps here, and I still do not know if I shall be able to get to Pondicherry to observe the second transit of Venus across the Sun on 3 June 1769 – the last one for more than a century. I hear conflicting news at our trading post on the war between France and England. I am considering Manila as an alternative observation post. Or I might travel from Manila to Pondicherry, through the eastern Indian seas, and the Sea of China, but I have no accreditation from the king for a sojourn in Spanish territory. I suspect that certain of my letters are not reaching France.

I have been meaning to describe to you a truly wonderful phenomenon in the seas here: at night, the water lights up. All of a sudden, the waves in the wake of our boats will glow, like a great triangle of light spreading out behind. An intense, profound brilliance that disappears just as quickly. We see it, too, in the crests of the little waves all around us. I think the light is produced by algae, or minute living creatures no bigger than the head of a pin. In the sea, the tiniest movement sparks their phosphorescence. I have tried observing the water with a magnifying glass, but I cannot make it out. I wish you were at my side. I should love to put my arm around your waist, breathe the scent of your hair, and feel your head against my shoulder as we sit and watch the shining sea together beneath the stars in the warm, salty evening breeze. I should like to collect a sample of this magical water and bring it back to France for you in a glass bottle, then shake it in the darkness of our bedchamber: the bottle would glow on the small table beside our bed. Our nuptials' witness.

I am very tired now, Hortense, my love. I feel my pen slip from the paper. I shall kiss your eyes and rest my head for a moment on your breast, lulled by your beating heart.

Guillaume

My dear confrère, Your Grace,

We have no news of Monsieur Le Gentil, your protégé. Have you received word from him?

César-François Cassini, Director of the Observatoire de Paris

My dear confrère,

You address me as 'confrère', and you flatter me more than you know – I am a mere duke, fascinated by the science of the heavens, but I am most pleased to accept the title you bestow, for the purpose of our correspondence. I received a letter from Monsieur Le Gentil one year ago, requesting funds. He writes that he has chosen to wait for the next transit of Venus across the Sun, in eight years' time, and that he will spend the intervening time studying the islands, their fauna and their flora, and mapping the seas to the best of his ability, for His Majesty the King.

Sincerely,
La Vrillière

My dear confrère, Your Grace,

It has been two years since our exchange of letters. My own letter to Monsieur Le Gentil is still without answer. I am told he is on his way to Manila, but others say his destination is the Isle de Bourbon.

César-François Cassini, Director of the Observatoire de Paris

My dear confrère,

I have no further news of Monsieur Le Gentil, not even whether he still lives. I received a letter from him last week – you may imagine my delight – but it was written two years ago, in Madagascar. Perhaps some of his letters have been lost in shipwrecks at sea. It worries me that nothing further has reached us.

La Vrillière

'And what about you, what are you reading at the moment?'

'I'm enjoying *Journey through the Seas of India* by Guillaume Le Gentil, a book from the eighteenth century.'

Luigi Nessi sat with his cocktail skewer poised in mid-air. He was silent for a moment, then lowered his glasses to look at Xavier more closely.

'Are you serious, young man?' he asked. 'Nobody knows that work or its author any more, apart from me, but I'm an old scholar from a different time... Who reads Le Gentil, these days, and knows his history?'

'I do,' said Xavier, as if making an apology. 'But I haven't finished the story yet, so don't tell me what happens, sir,' he added with a smile. Luigi Nessi was a man of old-fashioned elegance, with his three-piece grey suit, white goatee and pocket watch whose gold chain hung casually out of his jacket. He was very old, and his right hand was plagued with gentle tremors, betraying the onset of Parkinson's. But behind his large tortoiseshell glasses, his hazel eyes were still sharp.

*

Xavier and Alice had met at six o'clock on the dot, outside the carriage entrance to Luigi's Marais townhouse, near Rue des Blancs-

Manteaux. They had arrived almost at the same time; Xavier was just one minute late, which allowed him to observe and then approach Alice as he walked down the street, while she checked her phone in front of the house.

'You're right on time,' she said with a smile.

'It's a habit in my line of work,' Xavier explained.

'Shall we go in?' asked Alice, and she rang the video intercom.

There was silence, and then: 'Yes?' said a voice.

'It's Alice Capitaine and Xavier Lemercier,' she replied, and the door opened with a click onto a small courtyard, in the centre of which stood a plane tree which must have been planted during the days of the Ancien Régime, its trunk was so thick and gnarled. At the top of a flight of steps, which were flanked by stone sphinxes, a glass door opened to reveal the tall figure of a man in his fifties with slicked-back black hair. He came towards them and greeted them politely.

'Monsieur is waiting for you in the winter garden. Follow me, please.'

Alice and Xavier looked at each other and exchanged a conspiratorial smile. They let the butler guide them through a large, high-ceilinged hall, its floor paved with black-and-white marble tiles that together resembled a giant chessboard whose enormous pieces, made from jade or lapis lazuli, had been temporarily put away for the next time. Expensive furniture, Louis XV armchairs, and a large ebony-and-tortoiseshell cabinet were placed in positions that were anything but random. They passed through a library whose mahogany shelves stretched to the ceiling, the highest shelves requiring the use of a rolling ladder, its wood polished from years of use. The books, mostly ancient and leather-bound, their spines embossed with gold leaf, spread in their hundreds across the walls. An immense globe that could be spun at will stood on an iron stand, alongside a stuffed kangaroo two metres tall, which seemed to smile ironically at all the human knowledge on the shelves before its motionless muzzle. The butler went ahead of them without a word, and they followed him next into a large winter garden; the June sunshine streamed through its domed greenhouse roof. There were so many flowers and plants it would have taken several hours to count them all. Xavier noticed a bed of anthuriums, while Alice commented on some carnivorous plants whose heavy, slender pitchers seemed to hang in mid-air. Just after a purple hibiscus they spotted the zebra, and standing by its side, walking stick in hand, the master of the house: Luigi Nessi di Lugano. The butler disappeared soundlessly.

'Darling Alice with the fairy hands, thank you for coming all the way to see me,' he welcomed her before ceremoniously kissing her hand.

'Luigi, you are a prince in his palace. Thank you for welcoming us,' Alice replied. 'This is Xavier Lemercier.'

'Hello and welcome, Monsieur Lemercier,' Luigi shook his hand. 'We'll have an aperitif in the garden, but first: your protégé in his kingdom!' he exclaimed, pointing towards the zebra with his cane. Alice gently approached the animal and ran her fingers over his short crest of a mane and over his left ear before moving down towards his shining muzzle.

'He looks magnificent in the winter garden,' she said.

Xavier came closer and looked into the animal's eyes, which seemed so alive that he was almost waiting for them to blink. He thought of the first time he had seen it: from far away, through the telescope, through an anonymous window. Since then, the window was no longer unknown, and he stood by the side of the woman who lived there, meeting the zebra once more amid the decor of a seventeenth-century Parisian townhouse that was as fabulous as it was immaculate. They had come so far in such a short time, he thought, and Alice's unexpected invitation to accompany her to this place made him think that maybe something could happen between them. Their children already got along to the point that Esther had given Olivier a present, which still remained a mystery. Xavier hesitated to put any hint of a shared future into words, still less picture it in his mind's eye, and yet he had a lightness of heart that he hadn't felt for a long time.

'Was it you who decided to put it there, Luigi?'

'Oh no,' he replied. 'That's always been his place. We are in my grandfather's Parisian house; he's the one who brought the zebra here in 1886.'

'Brought… you mean to say alive?' asked Xavier.

'Absolutely,' Luigi replied. 'Look, this is him,' he added, pointing to a small frame hung on the wall which contained a black-and-white photo. Alice and Xavier approached it to see a man in his sixties, every bit as elegant as their host, but stouter and with a moustache, standing beside a zebra. They both looked proudly at the camera.

'My grandfather was an avid hunter. Come into the garden,' he said, taking Alice by the arm with authority and leading the way. 'He had the opportunity to do what we call a "safari" these days. He brought back several trophies which would be forbidden today, so much for the better, but most importantly he came back with the zebra. He was only small when my grandfather found him, and he had a broken leg. My grandfather took him in and nursed him back to health, but the zebra was lame, and his chances of survival were slim. He grew fond of the zebra, so Alberto, my grandfather, decided to bring him back and give him a home in the garden of his Parisian townhouse. He named him Anatole. When he brought him back here, I don't think the zebra was much bigger than a greyhound, he grew up in this very garden,' said Luigi as they descended a stone staircase that looked over a large garden, which Xavier estimated to cover 800 square metres.

'In his day, the zebra would walk around and attend receptions and summer parties – there are photos in the family album. When he died, Alberto was so distraught that he asked a taxidermist to immortalise his beauty, and he then placed him in the winter garden. And you, my dear,' he said to Alice. 'You have given him a new lease of life. Sit, my friends,' said Luigi as they approached a yellow domed gazebo, underneath which a beautiful table was laid with crystal glasses, ice buckets and three armchairs. Xavier felt he couldn't be far from heaven. It must look something like this, at least. They sat down on the chairs and the butler appeared with two trays bearing skewers of grilled lobster. He offered them a choice between a Campari spritz, a glass of Chevalier-Montrachet or a glass of Roederer Cristal. Alice opted for the white wine, as did Xavier, and Luigi nodded.

'Very good choice – the only choice, in fact. The other two were just decoys,' he smiled playfully. 'The Chevalier-Montrachet is the best white wine in the world,' he added, and the butler filled their glasses with a pale gold liquid that shone in the sunlight. They raised their glasses and enjoyed the dry white Burgundy with its rare and prized mineral flavour. In the warm June air, the conversation ambled pleasantly along to the subject of the dodo that Alice had just finished, and she showed them some photos she had taken on her phone. Then the conversation turned to real-estate prices.

'I'm thinking of moving,' said Alice. 'Xavier has shown me an apartment I'm very interested in.'

Upon hearing about Xavier's profession, Luigi told him that his daughter, who lived in Milan, was looking for a pied-à-terre in Paris, and if Xavier knew of anything, he should let him know. Then the conversation turned to what they were reading. Luigi was passionate about travel writing, and was reading a book about the most unexpected journeys: a quantum mathematics thesis on parallel universes. According to the theory it proposed, we exist within a multitude of similar universes which reflect one another like two mirrors positioned face to face, but containing different variables. The variables, ranging from death to a different profession or a different wife, were the result of our choices in life. Everybody was left mystified by this prospect of quantum possibilities that would transform us into hundreds of clones of ourselves, all taking very different paths. Still in the realm of the bizarre, though tinged with nineteenth-century romanticism, Alice was rereading Edgar Allan Poe as well as a very rare tract about lemurs that she had found on eBay, written in the eighteenth century by one Aldebert d'Arcourt, a complete unknown. Finally, it was Xavier's turn, and he mentioned the book by the king's astronomer, to Luigi's great surprise.

'Guillaume Le Gentil de La Galaisière…' Luigi repeated. 'It's been a long time since I've spoken that name. I had the first edition of *Journey through the Seas of India* – I parted ways with it when I sold my library.'

'Which year was that again, Luigi?' asked Alice.

'It was two thousand and three, November and December,' he said. 'Two complete catalogues at Sotheby's, seventeen hundred books. I only kept the ones that I still read regularly. What can I do? My daughters are not bibliophiles. I might as well pass my treasures on to other collectors while I'm still here. Returning to Le Gentil,' he said, addressing Xavier once more, 'it's strange that you bring him up. I was just thinking about him last week.' There was a silence, and Xavier looked at him with questioning eyes. 'I'm reading a scientific journal I subscribe to, and they mention the transit of Venus across the sun.'

'The one Guillaume Le Gentil was trying to see?' asked Xavier.

'No, the next one! The last for more than a century! It's going to happen in two weeks, on the sixth of June. I even set my watch,' he said, patting his jacket pocket. 'So I can follow it on the internet. We'll only be able to see the end of it from Paris, but it will definitely be visible.'

'The transit of Venus is happening again in two weeks?' Xavier asked, incredulous.

'Yes,' Luigi confirmed. 'At sunrise, for an hour. The next time Venus passes before the sun will be in twenty-one seventeen. You chose a good time to read his book,' he added with a smile. 'One question,' he continued, after taking a sip of white wine. 'What led you to Guillaume the astronomer? Are you an astronomy fanatic?'

'Oh no,' said Xavier, 'I'm no great star specialist. I'm more interested in heritage and architecture.'

'So why read Le Gentil, then? Do you like travel writing, perhaps?'

'I like his, yes, but it's mostly because of a chance encounter,' said Xavier, taking another sip of the Montrachet. 'I found Guillaume Le Gentil's telescope in the back of a cupboard in an apartment I sold a while ago. No one came to claim it, so I kept it and put it on my balcony—'

Xavier stopped abruptly. Luigi's face blurred before his eyes for a moment, and the light seemed more intense. He sensed Alice turning her head slowly towards him and felt her gaze on his profile. A silent look, as still as those of the fantastic animals that passed through her hands.

'It must be one of those copper telescopes on steel legs, with the astronomer's name engraved on it,' Luigi continued.

'Yes…' Xavier's voice was barely audible. 'That's right.'

'That's marvellous!' Luigi cried. 'You'll be able to see the eclipse from your own telescope! You can avenge Guillaume Le Gentil! Although I won't tell you the end of the story,' he said, raising his glass to Xavier.

'Don't tell me,' said Xavier, with a quiet sigh. Alice had not moved, and he didn't dare look at her.

'He's perfect,' Luigi whispered in Alice's ear as he accompanied them to the front door. Alice gave him a questioning look. 'Your boyfriend,' he said, indicating Xavier, who was walking behind them. 'Cultured, well brought up, and he's reading Le Gentil. He's perfect, believe me.'

'Luigi,' she said, with a sad smile. 'Thank you for this beautiful afternoon. Never change, maestro,' she said to him, placing her hand on his arm. Xavier came to thank him, and then they found themselves on the pavement once more, as the carriage door closed with a click. Alice and Xavier stood side by side in silence for a moment, then she raised her eyes to him, and they stared at one another.

'It's your apartment,' Alice said quietly. 'You showed me your apartment. I had you come to my house. You can see through my windows from your house. You have an antique telescope on your terrace. Have you been spying on me?'

Xavier didn't have the strength to reply.

'I don't know who you are. You scare me. Let's leave it at that.' She walked off along the pavement.

Xavier remained in front of the carriage door, as if petrified. How could heaven have turned so quickly into hell? With one sentence, one word: 'telescope'. If he hadn't brought up the telescope, Alice would still be smiling at him and they would be walking side by side down the street, discussing Luigi's marvellous townhouse and the astonishing story of the zebra, Anatole. Everything would be different. Luigi Nessi was right with his quantum theories: there must be another universe in which Xavier had skilfully evaded the question about his sudden interest in *Journey through the Seas of India*. Yes, perhaps that universe existed, but he wasn't in it.

He had lost Alice. He had lost everything.

My dear confrère, Your Grace,

Seven years have passed since Monsieur Le Gentil set sail. Members of the Académie are suggesting his Chair be passed to someone else. Members of his family wish us to acknowledge his death formally so that they may inherit his Estate on a presumption of death, though no body has been found. A delicate matter.

Our Academician has disappeared without trace.

César-François Cassini, Director of the Observatoire de Paris

My dear confrère,

I do not know what to say in response to your letter. Either Monsieur Le Gentil is alive, and will one day return home to France, or he is with God. Only time will tell.

La Vrillière

My dear confrère,

I have just received, by the dawn mail coach, a most remarkable seashell, very carefully wrapped. It seems that an accompanying letter has been mislaid. Who other than Monsieur Le Gentil would send such a curiosity? I take this as proof that he is still alive. I shall place it in the church, at the feet of St Guillaume, and give instructions for prayers to be said for his well-being.

La Vrillière

My dear confrère,

An eternity since we corresponded.

A man whom I believe to be of good faith, a merchant and a traveller, something of an adventurer for our trading post in the East Indies, has brought news of another man, a stranger to India, white-skinned, speaking French, who arrived on a ship from Manila. He is said to be staying in the ruins of the French palace in Pondicherry, with an armed guard of fiercely loyal Hindus.

My man told me he saw the fellow from the gardens, on a balcony, wearing a blue French frock coat with gilt buttons, and his hair very long, all the way down his back. His guards chased my man away.

Might this be our Monsieur Le Gentil?

La Vrillière

The city had sweltered in a muggy heat for the past three days. Guillaume woke sluggishly in the governor's great four-poster bed. The mosquito screen was disintegrating rapidly. On his arrival, there had been just a single slash, the length of a dagger's blade, but now a section more than a yard in length fluttered on the evening breeze, like a friendly ghost. He sat up against his pillows and blinked several times, as if he had been gazing too long at the sun. After the seas of India, here was India itself, and he had been here almost a year. His passage via Manila had been difficult indeed. The city was well situated for astronomical observations, and tolerably comfortable, but the Spanish authorities had received no letter of introduction ahead of his arrival. He carried his letter of accreditation, signed by His Majesty Louis XV, as always, but it had proved of little use and had perhaps even counted against him.

*

The Spaniards had greeted him with suspicion from the moment he landed: the eight chests of seashells had been opened, and every drawer inspected. The customs official, a large man with a moustache, kept nodding and shaking his head as if the collection of shells concealed some other, far darker purpose. They had checked all the drawers for hidden compartments under a false bottom. His astronomical instruments had been mistaken at first for outlandish weaponry of some sort, that could be assembled and dismantled as required, so as to carry out a heinous assassination. Try as he might, Guillaume failed to convince the King of Spain's men that he was on a mission to observe the next transit of Venus across the disc of the sun. When his translator – a gaunt, elderly man named Pedro, with long, trailing moustaches – informed him that the guards were insisting he describe this Venus, and take them to meet her straightaway, Guillaume realised the challenge he faced. He spent several hours at the harbourmaster's office explaining that he was an astronomer sent by the King of France to observe the first transit in 1761 and to calculate from it the distance between the Earth and the sun.

Pedro translated the customs official's response in his approximation of French: 'He says that if you came to observe something that happened in 1761, you have no place hereabouts seven years after the event.'

'Tell him that I missed the first transit and that I am waiting for the second, next year.'

His translated reply caused the Spanish soldier to burst out laughing, followed by a flurry of swearing, rendered by Pedro in simple terms: 'This I cannot translate for the envoy of His Majesty the King of France.'

It was only later that day, early in the afternoon, that an emissary of the French ambassador to Manila had come to the astronomer's rescue. It was all a misunderstanding. The Spanish were tetchy and nervous, because secret naval documents had been stolen the day before yesterday, and it was rumoured a French spy had taken them. Guillaume was released and took up residence in the city. A sizeable train of porters carried his eight chests of seashells, and he devoted himself to his usual astronomical observations, together with his succinct descriptions of what he saw of daily life going on around him: the beliefs, customs and mores of the lands through which his astonishing voyage had taken him over the past seven years. He wrote everything down in a huge bound volume. Manuscript pages alternated with maps, diagrams and drawings of the temples and sacred figures he had seen. He had given the work a provisional title: *Journey through the Seas of India*.

He cherished two fond memories of Manila. The first was his meeting with Don Esteban Roxas y Melo, the canon of the city's cathedral, a Peruvian born in Lima, and himself an amateur astronomer, with whom Guillaume had been able to talk science, in French. Father Melo thought that Guillaume had gone home to France after the first transit, then returned to the seas of India. He found it hard to believe, as Guillaume assured him, that he had chosen to stay in the region and wait.

'Time passes differently here,' Guillaume had explained.

'I believe you, but still, eight years is a long time,' Father Melo had repeated, several times over. On his last day, the two men had taken their leave of one another. The canon had decided to observe the eclipse from Manila, and Le Gentil had settled on his original destination: Pondicherry, the East Indies trading post, now liberated from the English at last.

His second distinct memory of Manila was of a fishing expedition for giant clams, in which he was accompanied by the canon. The fishermen had found an enormous clam on the seabed in the bay, like those used for baptismal fonts in church naves, and the discovery provoked no small excitement on board the boat. Bringing it to the surface, tied with ropes, proved a difficult operation in which Guillaume assisted, under the astonished gaze of Father Melo.

'I see you've learned a great deal about how the savages live here,' he said, when Guillaume returned to his side, bare-chested, after heaving on the rope with the rest of the crew, who had thanked him with a series of hearty slaps on the back.

'As I see it,' Guillaume began, 'there are no savages, only men, who approach the natural world differently from ourselves.' He sat down on a sack full of ropes. 'Look at that sailor, all covered in tattoos, with his back to us.' He pointed to a man decorated from his hips to the nape of his neck with twin red dragons facing each other off, as if ready to fight. 'That man knows as much about the seabed as you or I do about the stars. We are each as learned as the other, in our respective fields. I would go so far as to say that his domain is perhaps more essential than ours, because his brings home food. Our observations have never given anyone a square meal.'

'Science is the food of the intellect,' objected Father Melo.

'Granted,' said Guillaume, 'but taste the grilled flesh of this clam, and you may change your mind.'

Back at port, the fishermen had extracted the huge mollusc using a long sabre, then cut a sizeable chunk for Guillaume, as thanks for his help aboard the boat. Curious onlookers gathered around the huge shell, and Guillaume regretted that he could not take it with him in one of his chests. The fishermen lit a fire on the harbourside, then placed an iron grill over it, laden with the sizzling chunks of clam, which they ate skewered on the blades of their knives. Guillaume took out his own, made to his order by the smith on Isle de France. He shared his meal with the canon.

'Such a delicacy, is it not?' said Guillaume. 'I had never eaten clam meat before I came here.'

His fellow astronomer nibbled his share warily, with a wince of regret. The salty, tender, grilled flesh reminded Guillaume of the delicious *lambis* he had eaten in Madagascar. Instinctively, he felt for the pocket of his waistcoat: the pink pearl was still there, together with the scrap of stardust he had collected on the deck of the *Berryer*.

*

When he had landed at last on the Coromandel coast, after seven years, he had struck the ground in the port several times with the heel of his shoe. This was no dream; he had truly arrived. The clap of black leather on stone was his proof. It had taken seven years, and a war, for him to finally set eyes on Pondicherry. And what he saw distressed him at first: the city lay half in ruins. Fierce fighting between the English, French and a host of local factions had reduced a fair portion of the splendid East Indies trading post to ashes. From Manila, Guillaume had written to the new governor of Pondicherry to announce his arrival. The reply had come in the person of an Indian youth wearing a brooch shaped like a white lily, in the buttonhole of his white linen coat.

'I have waited at the harbourside every day for the past eight days to see your ship come into port. Welcome to India, Monsieur Le Gentil de La Galaisière.' He greeted Guillaume with a bow of his head.

Guillaume returned the gesture and replied: 'Please, call me Guillaume.'

They found porters for the eight chests of seashells, which they piled onto a cart like sarcophagi, while the Indian youth, whose name was Shakri, invited Guillaume to follow him to a small, curiously shaped carriage with an open top, pulled by a donkey. They seated themselves, and the astronomer beheld the half-ruined streets. Some of the bigger buildings were still standing, their spice-coloured walls resplendent in the sunlight, while others, just a few paces away, had been blown wide open or were coated in soot from a housefire. They passed a garrison of the king's soldiers. The French flag, flying among the sunlit ruins while the inhabitants went about their business clad in richly coloured drapery, was a striking sight – a symbol – from a land so far away. As everywhere on his journey, Guillaume marvelled at the colours of the drapery, veils and turbans worn by the local men and women – deep pinks, purples and blues so bright he felt inclined to screw up his eyes; saffron yellows that dazzled like the sun. Shakri pointed to a large, pale-pink palace that looked as if it too had suffered in the fighting. The building stood on higher ground, overlooking the city.

'See there, Guillaume. That is where His Excellency the Governor will accommodate you. His former palace.'

'A most excellent observation post,' Guillaume replied.

That evening, Governor Jean Law de Lauriston received him in his temporary palace. They discussed the war over a meal of chicken cooked in a distinctively flavoured mint sauce. The new governor seemed as weary of the local cuisine as he was of his mission. He told Guillaume that he could make use of the palace as he wished. He would send his water-carriers up every morning and evening, and they would bring food, too. He entrusted his own guide, Shakri, to Guillaume, together with five armed guards: the city was not safe at the moment. He presented him with a large, double-barrelled pistol, bullets and a pouch of gunpowder.

'This is for your personal use. Keep it loaded, and never go anywhere without it.'

*

Guillaume lifted the mosquito net. His gaze fell on the pistol, which lay on his bedside table while he slept. His guards were asleep on cushions laid directly on the floor. One of them opened an eye, cat-like, then closed it again. Guillaume walked across to the huge, colonnaded terrace. Two of the pillars were shattered. The entire city lay stretched out below. The sun was at its height. In five days' time, the second and last transit of Venus in his lifetime would take place, across its burning disc.

Everything was ready. Guillaume had taken over the half-ruined palace more easily than he had imagined. The entire ground floor was occupied by the five guards, who took their meals there and chatted among themselves before coming upstairs to sit around on cushions and attend to the astronomer. Motionless, they kept watch in silence, studying his silhouette through half-closed eyes. Guillaume had prepared everything, beginning with the camera obscura, which he had carefully set up next to a window. It was shrouded in heavy, coloured silks so that no daylight could enter, except through a tiny optical hole in the outer casing. On the opposite wall, freshly painted in white, the sun's disc would be projected, a good sixteen inches in diameter. A perfect circle of light, its outer rim all aflame, marked for the moment by nothing but the cast shadows of distant birds. Tomorrow, the image of the sun would be traversed in real time by a black marble: Venus. The observation would last for several hours, and Guillaume would be able to move at will from his telescopes to the projection on the wall to take the most accurate measurements of the phenomenon. He had found some old music stands and placed one beside each of his instruments. Each would hold papers, ink pots and quill pens, so that he could note down his astronomical observations as easily as possible. While his guards watched impassively, he practised moving from one post to the next, sliding across the marble floor like an ice skater. The set-up was perfect: when his eye tired of observing the transit through the copper telescope, he would move across to the projection, then come back to Margissier's large spyglasses, or the eyepiece of the huge, fifteen-foot nautical telescope.

Eight years spent waiting for this precise moment. Thousands of seashells collected and inventoried; thousands of fish caught, from Isle de France to the China Sea, fish he had prepared, boiled, eaten, and shellfish, too, species that no one in France had cracked open, even in their dreams. Eight long years. Hundreds of pots of ink had been mixed and transformed into writings or mathematical formulae or diagrams of the heavens, on thousands of pages. The same ink, the same quills had traced the contours of the coastline, lapped by the infinite blue of the sea. Eight years of tireless hard work and unexpected leisure would culminate tomorrow in the ultimate reward: the second transit of Venus, and the last for 105 years.

Guillaume moved once again from his telescopes to the camera obscura, watched through half-closed eyes by two of his semi-recumbent guards. A small bell rang out in the hallway. Time for his massage. Three times a week, a practitioner came to administer the singular, delightful ritual that he had discovered on the governor's recommendation. There was nothing like it in France; indeed, it seemed highly likely that his masseuse would have been forbidden from plying her trade, on moral grounds. Here in India, however, massage was practised purely as a kind of philosophy of relaxation and well-being. There could be no question of touching the person performing the massage, and she concentrated solely on specific, authorised parts of the body. Under her expert touch, the mind achieved a state of relaxation comparable to that of the muscles in the back or the legs, kneaded and pummelled by her art. The first time the governor had told him about massage, Guillaume had consigned the practice to the list of curious customs he had compiled on his travels. He must experience it first-hand, so that his *Journey through the Seas of India* – if ever it saw publication from the royal press – would truly be a reliable, genuine work of reference. He had asked Shakri to recommend a masseuse who could come to the palace. The first young woman who presented herself was none other than Shakri's sister. She had a cousin who was a masseuse, too, and the cousin had a friend who knew another masseuse. Before anyone had laid hands on him, before Guillaume was able to translate that strange word, 'massage', into physical sensation, he had concluded that most of the women in India were skilled in the practice. Perhaps massage was reciprocal? He noted, 'The people of the Indies massage one another.'

The young woman had brought with her a large bag filled with silk cushions of various sizes, and every imaginable colour. Guillaume was asked to remove his shirt, his breeches and his stockings, and to keep only his undergarments. The masseuse had arranged the cushions on a woven mat that she had unrolled on the floor. Guillaume was invited to lie down on his stomach. There were two small cushions for his elbows and hands, two others for his knees and two for his feet; one large, flat cushion was laid under his torso. The position was supremely comfortable. The masseuse lit incense sticks that gave off a strong peppery aroma, quite different from cathedral incense at home in France. Then she spoke a few words in her own language and poured warm, scented oil from a flask onto the astronomer's body. Her hands worked rhythmically up and down his back, their regular movement interspersed with occasional, carefully calculated pressure on individual muscles. It felt delightful. 'How have we never thought to massage one another in France?' he pondered, as he gradually entered a state of ecstasy comparable to that which he had experienced on his first swim in Isle de France. His legs, the nape of his neck, his hands and feet, shoulders and arms, his whole body, were massaged for more than two hours, and it seemed at times as if he had almost slipped out of consciousness.

Rather than confine his astonishing initiation into the art of massage to a mere footnote on the traditions of India, he chose to take it forward, for his own well-being. Since when, masseuses came regularly to the palace, two or three times a week, announcing their arrival with a tinkle of the little bell in the hallway. Today's practitioner entered the room, escorted by one of the guards. She bowed her head to Guillaume, who did the same. The ritual laying-out of the large and small cushions began, and Guillaume removed his shirt. The next time he lay down for his massage, Venus would have come and gone.

'This is very presumptuous of me, I am aware. I shouldn't be here, disturbing you. Please forgive me, Luigi,' said Alice, running her hand through her hair nervously. The two of them were sitting in the garden of the collector's townhouse, the very place where they had taken an aperitif five days previously to visit the zebra in his eternal abode. Except this time, there were only two of them. One guest was missing, and he was the subject of this visit. Luigi Nessi had the butler bring coffee in a beautiful silver-gilt set, and the man with the slicked-back hair poured it into two cups which sparkled in the sunshine, before disappearing soundlessly back towards the steps. Alice seemed very distressed and stared at the gilded saucer of her cup without saying anything. Luigi settled himself more comfortably in his chair and looked kindly at her for a long time before she lifted her eyes to his.

'Alice with the fairy hands,' he began. 'Tell me what could possibly be troubling that pretty face. You sent me a very mysterious email, ending with the words "I need the advice of a wise man who has lived. Luigi, you're the only one who can help me." For a start, *bellissima*, I don't know if I am as wise as all that,' he said with a conspiratorial smile. 'But I certainly have lived, it's true. I'm very old, and I have seen and heard many things. As for advice, I don't know that I will be very good at it, but I can always give you my opinion if you wish to hear it.'

Alice closed her eyes. 'I don't know where to begin,' she said.

'By drinking this coffee, which I had brought over from Florence,' said Luigi, and Alice smiled in reply before bringing the cup to her lips. Luigi did the same, this time using his left hand, the fourth finger of which boasted a large ring with a red stone. His right hand shook on his thigh like an injured animal. He noticed the look on her face. 'I'm going to have a glove made, a silk one lined with lead, to make that blasted hand stay still. I found an artisan in Venice who can make it.'

Alice met his eyes. 'You're brave, Luigi.'

'I don't have a choice,' he said resignedly. 'My Parkinson's is getting worse. They give me a year, two at most.' There was a silence between them. 'Do you know what is in this ring?' he asked, gesturing to his left hand. Alice shook her head slowly. 'Poison,' he said. 'It's an old piece of jewellery, a gadget, like the Borgia family used to wear. One day, before this illness completely destroys me,' he said quietly, 'I will open the bezel of this ring and pour its contents into my glass. My death will have all the symptoms of a stroke. No one will know, not even my children. Only you will know what I have done.'

Alice looked at him in silence. 'Luigi… why are you confiding this in me?'

He smiled gently. 'Because you are going to tell me a secret that torments you, so I have told you one of mine. Now we're even.'

Alice closed her eyes. 'You are a true prince,' she said softly.

'A very old prince,' Luigi replied. 'And I'm listening…'

Alice took a breath. 'Xavier,' she began.

'The man who knows Guillaume Le Gentil,' said Luigi.

'Yes,' said Alice. 'Him. I trusted him, I found him so charming, so considerate, I told myself… He is divorced, and he has his son every other weekend; my daughter and I are alone. I told myself that perhaps our meeting wasn't a coincidence. That at this point in our lives, we would each find someone and live happily ever after. I thought both our paths had been strewn with sadness and difficulty and that we could… Our children seem to get on well. I find Xavier charming and…'

'And?' Luigi prompted gently.

'And now I find it's not so. I don't know who to talk to. I don't have friends close enough to confide in. I wanted to talk to my grandmother, but she isn't here any more. My parents divorced many years ago; my father lives in England and we haven't spoken for a long time. My mother is no longer with us. As for my sister, we've never got on; she lives in Germany.'

'So, it was easier to come and see Luigi in Paris,' said the Italian kindly. 'What happened?'

Alice closed her eyes and took a deep breath. 'You asked him how he knew about that astronomer, and he told you he had found his telescope, an old telescope. Well, Xavier showed me an apartment which has everything I was looking for, and in that apartment there was an old telescope on the balcony that matches the description of the one belonging to the astronomer. You can see the whole city, and better yet, my windows. That apartment…'

'It's his,' finished Luigi.

'Yes,' Alice sighed.

'And he didn't tell you it was his?'

'No,' said Alice. 'He didn't say anything. He lied to me and told me he had taken it on recently.'

Luigi nodded slowly. 'Why do you want to move?' he asked.

'It's my husband's apartment. It's where I lived with him, and when he died, I inherited it and stayed there, among my memories, with Esther. The apartment is wonderful, I love it dearly, and I love the neighbourhood too, but the weight of the past gets heavier over the years. I was wrong: I thought it would get lighter over time, but in fact it's the opposite. The longer I live there, the less I understand why I am still there. I didn't want to sell it because it was the last thing connecting me to him. I thought it would be heartless to sell it. It would be like betraying him, selling what's left of us, forgetting the past, in a way. I don't know if I'm making sense.'

'You are. I understand you perfectly. So, you contacted Xavier to look for an apartment?'

'Yes, I looked for estate agents in the neighbourhood by geographic proximity, and his was the first.'

Luigi thought for a moment. 'What pushed you to consider leaving your apartment?'

Alice was silent for a moment, staring at the gilded saucer. 'My last relationship,' she said, 'ended like all the others. We didn't understand one another, we couldn't make it work as a couple. I… I live with Esther, all the time. I'm alone with her. My husband's parents are no longer with us, and I have no one I can entrust her to. It's the two of us, we are like a couple. My days revolve around her school pick-up; my weekends, my holidays – it's all about the two of us. To come to your house the other day I had to ask my neighbour to look after her, but I only do that rarely. I don't think there's room for a man in my life. It's never, ever worked.'

'What did he do, this last man?' Luigi asked.

'He was in technology,' said Alice. 'The internet. Among other things, he had a well-known meditation site. I even did some readings for it. He said my voice was serious but gentle and it worked very well. I read texts that psychologists had written but didn't want to read themselves. I enjoyed it, it was fun, and relaxing.' She paused before continuing. 'Our children didn't get along. His daughter hated Esther, and so she hated me too. I think she saw me as a woman who had come to steal her father. I've been through that many times. It's endless, it's exhausting.'

'And with Xavier?' Luigi asked thoughtfully.

'I trusted him. Very quickly, I don't even know why. I had him view my apartment for a valuation. When I think about that now… He told me about his son who he only sees every other weekend. He saw the zebra in my living room, and when I told him what I do, he asked if he could come to the museum with his son, and it was a wonderful afternoon. I didn't give much away, but our children got along so well, and he seemed truly interested in my profession.

Everything seemed so perfect! I hadn't been happy like that in years. The next day, I checked the weather because I thought it had been sunny. In fact, it had been overcast but I remembered it as sunny,' Alice finished.

'That is the way of love,' Luigi murmured, and took a sip of coffee. 'The telescope,' he continued, putting down his cup. 'Did you talk about it after you left here?'

Alice nodded.

'What did you say?'

'I asked him if he had spied on me with it, I asked him if it was his apartment, I told him he scared me, and then I left.'

'What did he say?'

'Nothing. He looked terrified.'

'He didn't say anything at all?'

'He wrote to me,' Alice admitted, lowering her gaze.

'Let me read it,' said Luigi. Alice looked at him questioningly. 'The letter – I'm sure you have it with you,' he said, smiling.

Alice bent down to her bag and took out an envelope, which she handed to Luigi. He lowered his tortoiseshell glasses and took a magnifying glass from his pocket, before unfolding the letter.

Paris, June 2012

Alice,

'Let's leave it at that,' you said to me before disappearing into the crowd. 'You scare me,' was the sentence just before. I must have written hundreds of letters and thrown them in the bin before starting this one, and I still don't know if I can do it – putting it in an envelope, attaching a stamp and posting it through a letter box seems impossible.

I will start by telling you the truth. Yes, I did get the king's astronomer's telescope from an apartment that I sold, and I have no idea what it could possibly have been doing there. I didn't keep it to observe the lives of others from my terrace, but for my son, so we could look at the stars and the moon together. Yes, I looked at you too, Alice. One day the telescope's view fell on your window, and you were on the balcony, tearing up a piece of paper and letting the pieces flutter away. You were dressed in black, and your hair was blowing in the wind. I thought you were beautiful, and intriguing, and the following days I pointed the telescope in the direction of your balcony again. I sometimes saw you, and sometimes I didn't; I never saw your daughter.

For me, you were 'the woman on the balcony', or 'the woman with the zebra', because I saw it briefly through your window and I have to admit I didn't think it was stuffed. In fact, I didn't think at all. I didn't understand what I was looking at. Perhaps it would all have ended there. I thought you were beautiful and unattainable in this huge city. Perhaps that would have been enough. But then you came through the door of the agency. You cannot imagine what went through my mind when I saw you before me. Something extraordinary was happening, and yet you came to me with the most normal of requests: to value your apartment. I don't even know how I managed to get out of my chair and accompany you to your house. Everything had become real, you really existed, you were walking by my side, and we were talking to each other. You were no longer a silent image in the round frame of the lens. And while we walked to your apartment, I daydreamed that we were together and this was the marvellous magic of our everyday life, walking next to each other in the street, talking.

It was like a fairy tale. You had me view your apartment, where the zebra I had seen from my terrace materialised before my eyes. You told me about yourself and about your daughter. My profession is unique: I enter into the lives of others, for a brief moment, then I disappear once the sale has completed. I know the city and its neighbourhoods. I have the keys to apartments that I can open at will, but everything is temporary, and none of it belongs to me. I have the power to open the doors of so many properties, and yet I see no doors in my own life. This time, I didn't want it to end. I don't know why or how we fall in love, Alice, but I did, I beg you to believe me. When you told me about your possible departure to Washington, I saw the likelihood of soon losing you without ever having told you I loved you. I think I panicked at the thought. I think the visit to the museum with our children convinced me of the strange decision to offer you my apartment. That day, you gave me one of the most beautiful afternoons I've had in a long time. Everything was so perfect, I could barely believe it was real. We got along well, we were surrounded by those still, friendly animals, and our children were gladly chatting away. If that isn't happiness, then I don't know what is.

Regarding my apartment, it was a crazy idea, a sudden impulse, the need to act and act fast so as not to lose you. I know these words are ridiculous; it's my fault, and mine alone, that my enthusiasm backfired. I couldn't decide whether or not to tell you it was my apartment, and to offer to exchange apartments in a sale; you would buy mine, and I would buy yours. I flipped a coin because I didn't know what else to do. Tails, I tell you, heads, I don't. It was heads. That was that and I lost you, in that moment. I am so sorry for the pain I have caused you and for the disappointment that I saw in your eyes after that beautiful afternoon with your Italian friend. I don't think I understand life at all. It's a cruel game that I don't have the instructions for.

Please don't remember me as a horrible liar. I'm just a poor boy, shy and clumsy, who never knew how to go about life.

I'll return to Guillaume Le Gentil, whose memoirs I am reading. His life was just a quest in which he constantly missed that which he was searching for. Unlike me, however, he had a beautiful journey.

I'll miss you always. I am inconsolable.

Xavier

Luigi Nessi placed his magnifying glass on the table, carefully put the letter back in the envelope and handed it to Alice, who put it in her bag. They looked at each other.

'How many birds have you done for me?'

'Thirty-two, Luigi,' Alice replied.

'How many kangaroos?'

'Just one,' she smiled.

'Until last week, we never met anywhere other than my offices.'

Alice agreed.

'I no longer have any offices; they've been sold, and I'm almost at the end of the road. I'd like to do something good in this life before I depart.' There was a pause. 'In the copy of *Journey through the Seas of India* that I sold, there was a very interesting letter from the astronomer, a letter to a woman whom I never identified, whom he called Hortense. In it he speaks of love, and above all of the "whims of the stars", the whims of Venus, the Goddess of Love. You two, Alice and Xavier, are the innocent victims of the whims of the stars.'

Alice shook her head in resignation, as though Luigi's words had not reassured her at all.

'Listen to me,' he said. 'My wife was called Graziella. We lived together for fifty-one years, God rest her soul, and, dear Alice, I did what you reproach Xavier for doing.'

Alice raised her eyes to him.

'A long time ago, when I was young, only eighteen years old, I saw Graziella for the first time in Piazza Navona, and I followed her. I was sitting on the edge of the fountain. It was the twenty-fifth of June 1947, at ten past four in the afternoon. She was walking with her father; women never went out alone in those days. I followed them for streets and streets, to their house, walking thirty metres behind them so they didn't see me. The next morning, I came back and hid at the corner of the street and followed her to her school. A few weeks later, I borrowed my father's hunting binoculars and I climbed a tree in the street outside the girls' school so that I could watch her in the yard. One time I got scolded by a fat man,' he said, smiling, lost in his memories. 'Finally, I managed to find out her name. She attended the high-society soirées where rich young men and women met. I arranged to join that circle and finally I managed to speak to her, "woo her", as we used to say.' He stopped for a moment, dreamy and quiet, while Alice held her breath. 'I never told Graziella that I followed her, that our meeting at the Fendi house was not the first. I never found the courage. Graziella never knew, but if I had told her and, what's more, written it down, I'm sure now that she would have seen it for what it was.'

'What was it?' Alice said quietly.

'Proof of love… I was no more responsible for crossing paths with Graziella than Xavier was for having spotted you through his telescope. I was not a sociopath or a pest, I just didn't know how to tell her I was in love with her. And I didn't want her to get away. I did what I could with what I had.'

'Why didn't he tell me it was his house? He lied to me, Luigi.'

'Perhaps he felt shame-faced, or took a gamble. Perhaps it was a wild impulse,' Luigi responded. 'He writes about it well in his letter. In any case, he would have told you if you were going to buy it.'

Alice's gaze moved over to a tree. She could think of nothing to say.

'Alice, life is short. Xavier is not a dangerous man. He's a dreamer. Don't let the dream pass you by. Wake up to reality, but remember the dream. In short: reply to him and watch the eclipse together with your children. It won't happen again for more than a century, Alice. In a century's time, what will remain of our loves, our sorrows, our emotions? The eclipse will happen in a few days and then it won't happen again anytime soon. And neither will love. That's what this old man has to say, since you asked my opinion. Anyway, what do you think of this coffee?'

'Thank you, Luigi,' sighed Alice, looking at him.

'For the coffee?' he smiled.

'For the coffee, and everything else,' she said, before placing her hand on his – the left hand, with the red ring.

The sky was clear, and Guillaume had not slept all night. Yesterday's massage had been most relaxing, but the day ahead promised to be extraordinary indeed. The instruments were ready, and the music stands were in position, close at hand. Shortly after the sun had risen, Guillaume opened the aperture of the camera obscura. The star's image was projected onto the white wall. Everything was going to plan. He had taken one of his cases and removed the black glass discs so as to screw them to the eyepiece of the copper telescope, the big lens of Margissier's eyepiece, and lastly the large nautical telescope. Each disc was perfectly adjusted, and Guillaume put his right eye up to each instrument: the sky appeared black as ink, and the sun formed a perfect white dot. In an hour's time he would unscrew the tops on his ink bottles, and the transit of Venus would begin. His guards woke. One of their number took up his post on the upper floor while the others ate breakfast below. Guillaume wasn't hungry. He poured himself a glass of water and drank it on the colonnaded terrace. The sky was a radiant blue. He closed his eyes for a moment, and the sun warmed his face as it climbed. Far off in the distance, he saw one of the fine sea mists that sometimes hung on the morning air before evaporating. He went back to his four-poster bed and lay down.

The next transit of Venus would take place in 1874. Who would be King of France? What wars would have come and gone? This half-ruined palace might not even exist in 105 years' time. What new stars and planets would mankind have discovered? Not a single living creature on the planet today would still be here. We shall all be dead, he thought. But then he remembered his tumble from the back of the giant tortoise, on the beach. Toussaint had told him that they could live for 200 years or more. Perhaps one of the tortoises on Isle de France will still be here, he thought, and the idea comforted him.

His thoughts on what might be, a hundred years hence, and the fleeting existence of living things, had occupied him for almost an hour. He rose, slipped his feet back into his silver-buckled shoes, ran his hands through his hair and tied it with a velvet ribbon, in a ponytail that hung down his back. He walked towards the terrace, to his telescopes, and glanced at the white wall facing the aperture of the camera obscura. The projected image of the sun, sixteen inches in diameter, had disappeared. He rushed to the balustrade and saw a sight that froze him as surely as the governor's blue morpho butterflies, pinned through their heads and mounted in their frames: the sea mist had risen, thicker than anything he had seen since arriving in Pondicherry almost a year ago. The gauzy pearl-grey fog filled the sky and the sun had disappeared. Guillaume stood rooted to the spot for an eternity of seconds. He felt violently dizzy and clung to one of the pillars. He closed his eyes, struggled to master his feelings, then stared again at the motionless haze. 'Lift…' he said quietly. 'Lift,' he said again, a little louder. 'Lift!' He was hollering now, gesturing towards the sky. 'Lift! Now, this minute!' His guard joined him on the terrace, clutching his sabre, ready to wield it and save the Frenchman from attack; but there was no one there. Only the astronomer, screaming at the sky. The guard was reassured – nothing had befallen the man under his own and his colleagues' protection. But the sight of him yelling at the sky was troubling. It seemed he had been gripped by a fit of panic, or rage, such as they had never seen in him before. Guillaume went to his bedside table and fetched his watch. It was time. The transit of Venus would begin in under a minute. The phenomenon of the 'black droplet' would appear. When the planet made first contact with the rim of the sun, the tiny black ball would appear to stretch and elongate before being silhouetted in its entirety against the burning disc. Guillaume shifted his gaze to the camera obscura. There was nothing on the wall but a blurred halo of light. No sun, still less a droplet of the planet Venus. It was taking place now – and the sky was as opaque as a painted grey wall.

The other guards had joined their colleague. They watched Guillaume closely. Some had ventured out onto the terrace and returned to the room behind to report what they had seen in their own language. They had little understanding of Guillaume's mission, but it was clear the astronomer's fevered state had been provoked by the persistent sea mist and the disappearance of the sun. Guillaume spent the first hour of the transit pacing back and forth, stepping out onto the terrace every ten minutes to stare with incredulity at the grey fog that showed no sign of lifting. The same ritual filled the second hour, though the guards noted that he went out to the terrace only twice. At the top of the third hour, Guillaume hurled his pillows at the wall where the eclipse should have appeared, tore down the mosquito net and threw himself onto his bed. At the end of the third hour, Shakri bent over him where he lay stretched out, pale and motionless as an effigy on a tomb.

'Is there a bottle of alcohol anywhere in the building?' the astronomer asked, feebly.

Shakri assured him he would procure one straightaway. He returned with a large, round-bellied bottle that held a drink with a taste similar to whisky. Guillaume drank a mouthful from the neck and thought of the last time he had felt the liquid fire on his tongue and throat, eight years earlier, aboard the *Sylphide*, upon missing the first transit. He decided against finishing the bottle, and handed it back to Shakri, then asked to be left alone for the next two hours, after which the transit of Venus in front of the sun would be at an end. In 120 minutes, it would all be over, and the skies above Pondicherry would be just the same.

Slumped in a large, velvet-upholstered armchair, his long hair tumbling over his shoulders, the astronomer stared at the tall windows, their filmy drapes floating on the air. Nothing would happen on this day. The sun was as absent as if it had been buried underground. He stared dully into space. 'What do you desire of me?' he murmured. 'What path are you showing me now?' For the first time in his life, talking to God brought no comfort, no help. Guillaume began to laugh. 'The keeper of the dodos said I would find love at my journey's end,' he said quietly. 'What love?!' His hollered question echoed around the marble walls and floor, then the palace fell silent again. Guillaume straightened up in his chair, then lay down on his bed once more, for the hour and a half that remained before the transit was complete.

He had fallen asleep, overcome with despair. A gentle warmth caressed his skin. Barely a minute passed before he half opened his eyes and was dazzled by a blinding light. He put a hand to his forehead, shielding his eyes from its intensity. The sun. It had just reappeared. At the very end of the eclipse. Guillaume staggered towards the terrace and pushed aside the tulle drapes to behold a cloudless blue sky and a bright, radiant sun shining with all its might. The fog that had persisted for hours was but a pale memory.

The gunshot shook his guards to their feet. They rushed up the grand staircase to the first floor, daggers and sabres drawn. The second gunshot was so deafeningly loud that it made them jump as they ran. But the Frenchman under their protection was neither wounded nor in any danger: it was he who had fired the shots. Guillaume had seized the big double-barrelled pistol given to him by the governor from its place on his bedside table, where it had lain ever since his arrival. Cautiously, the guards approached and found him standing on the terrace, his long hair blowing in the wind, as he tipped a generous charge of gunpowder into the barrels. He dropped in a couple of bullets, then pressed everything down with a stick of wood and prepared to fire again: he extended his arm, pointed the barrels of the gun at the sun, closed one eye, and pressed the trigger. The flintlock struck with a spark and a bullet shot out towards the star with a deafening blast, followed by a whiff of gunpowder. Guillaume repeated the operation and fired the remaining bullet.

The guards seated themselves on their cushions, cross-legged and motionless, while the astronomer continued firing at the sun and reloading his weapon until he had run out of ammunition.

Focus on your breathing as it goes in and out. Concentrate on your nostrils. Put aside the thoughts going through your mind. This is your time. You are with yourself.

The little gong sounded from the app on his phone. The meditation session with the male voice began. But Xavier couldn't put aside the thoughts going through his mind, let alone concentrate on his nostrils.

Lie down comfortably, back straight, feet flat, shoulders open, the voice continued. Ignoring these suggestions, Xavier was slumped in a living room chair, staring at the sliding doors of the terrace.

Breathe deeply in and out three times. Xavier breathed deeply in and out three times. Then the voice stopped, and silence fell in the room. The sun was already high in the blue sky, but nothing of this beautiful June morning had any effect on him.

What had happened these last few days? He had written to Alice and got no reply. He shouldn't have written. But now he had done it, not writing was no longer an option. It had been the right thing to do, but it didn't matter anyway because she had not responded.

The image of Alice walking away from him down the street came into his head constantly, several times a day, or an hour. Ten days had gone by. Ten days marked by happenings both large and small, both personal and professional, but none could compare to the intensity of Alice's sudden disappearance. The eighty-square-metre apartment with the view of the courtyard had sold in less than forty-eight hours.

A couple had come, the Baumanns. Xavier had given them a viewing in a gloomy voice that had surprised even himself: 'Bathroom, with a claw-footed tub… view of the courtyard. It's a good offering in the current market, on a quiet street.'

'Very good,' the man had said.

'It's just what we're looking for,' the woman had agreed. They had looked at each other and then at Xavier. 'We'll take it.'

'Excuse me?'

'We're going to buy it,' the man repeated, and Xavier nodded.

'Good, it's an excellent investment. Let's go back to the agency and we can sign the agreement.' That had been Thursday.

On Saturday, Olivier had opened Esther's present, the little bag with the coloured handles that she had attached to it. Xavier had seen Olivier, enthralled, pull out of the tissue paper… the stuffed flying fish. How could he tell Olivier that Alice no longer wanted to see his father? That he and Esther would probably never meet again, now that the girl had given him something that she prized above all else? Xavier was tormenting himself with this when his son came to stand before him, the flying fish in his right hand.

'I need to reply to Esther,' he began in a serious voice.

'Yes,' Xavier agreed, seriously.

'So, I need to use your computer to send her an email.'

'Excuse me?' said Xavier.

Olivier sat down on a chair and looked at his father with a degree of calm greater than all the meditation sessions imaginable.

'Esther and I worked out that something's going on with you and Alice. We don't know what and we don't want to know. So, we've been communicating by email.'

'Wait, wait,' said Xavier, thrown off by the information overload. 'You have an email account? Olivier, my eleven-year-old son, has an email account?'

'Yes,' Olivier confirmed. 'It's a Gmail account. I made it on Mum's computer. I use it when she's not in the room and I haven't told her about Esther.'

'And Esther has an email account, too?' sighed Xavier.

'Yes, Esther has an email account. She does the same as me, she uses the computer when her mum isn't in the room, because her mum doesn't want her to have an email account.'

Xavier closed his eyes and pinched his brow, thinking, but was there anything to think about? No, his eleven-year-old son had asked him a clear, specific question, and and there was nothing for him to do but admit defeat.

Olivier sat down in front of the computer.

'The password is…' Xavier began.

'I know it,' said Olivier.

'You know the password?'

'Yeah,' he said, shrugging. 'I've seen you type it in loads of times.' And he typed it in, opened a web page and connected to Gmail. Xavier began to wonder if his son had grown up too fast, then abandoned the thought as it would lead nowhere. The image of Alice walking away from him down the street came to mind again. He sat on the sofa while Olivier tapped at the keyboard.

'I wanted to suggest something to you,' Xavier said. 'But maybe you're no longer interested. The transit of Venus, which our astronomer friend missed, is happening again in five days, and it hasn't happened for more than a century. The next one will be in twenty-one seventeen.'

Olivier turned to his father. 'Brilliant! We absolutely have to watch it through the telescope, with Esther,' he said. Xavier put his head in his hands, trying to find an acceptable answer to give to his son. After a long minute of silence, an email arrived.

'Esther says that's great!'

'Olivier,' Xavier muttered.

'She also says you just have to sort things out and fall in love again. Now she's gone again because Alice came back into the room.'

Xavier looked fixedly at his son.

'It's up to you two to sort it out, not us,' Olivier said firmly, with a confidence that his father had never seen before.

'There's a problem though,' said Xavier, once the moment had passed. 'The transit of Venus is happening very early on a Wednesday morning, at sunrise. Your mum will need to let you stay here overnight, and there's no guarantee she will.'

'She'll let me,' Olivier said.

'How do you know?'

'Because if you ask her, she'll say no, but if I ask her, she'll say yes. Where are we going to see Venus from?'

'I don't know,' sighed Xavier. 'Maybe on the terrace.'

An email arrived on the computer.

'I'm going to ask Esther,' Olivier said, and Xavier got up to shut himself away in the kitchen before making dinner.

'She said she's going to think of somewhere special!' Olivier shouted from the living room.

'Croque-monsieur?' was Xavier's only reply. Making their favourite dinner, with no need to think about anything other than the pieces of toasted bread, ham and tomatoes, might help clear his head.

'Oh yeah, croque-monsieur!' Olivier said approvingly. 'I'm going to look up some things about Venus. Call me when it's ready.'

When his mother came to pick him up on Sunday night, there had been no progress on the future observation of the transit of Venus – with or without Esther. Nor on the location.

'Olivier seems different,' Céline said, looking at Xavier, while their son was in his room gathering his things. 'He's changed,' she continued. 'He suddenly seems much more mature.'

Xavier agreed, nodding his head. 'Maybe he's in love?' he suggested.

Céline rolled her eyes. 'You can't be in love at eleven years old. And if he was, he would have told me,' she said, shrugging. Xavier said nothing, and Olivier returned with his rucksack.

'I'm going to watch the transit of Venus with Dad's telescope, it's a really rare event, it won't happen again for a century,' he announced immediately.

'The transit will happen very early on Wednesday morning before school, at sunrise,' Xavier explained.

'I need to stay here Tuesday night and then Dad will take me to school.'

'What's all this?' Céline protested straightaway.

'I have to hand in my French essay about "a recent memory",' Olivier continued steadily.

'Yes,' said his mother.

'I'm going to write about the transit of Venus across the sun. It'll be much more original than anyone else's.' Olivier paused, looking at his mother, then turned to his father.

Well played, thought Xavier, trying not to show the pride he felt at his son's negotiation skills.

'Fine, okay,' Céline sighed. 'Your father and I will sort out the details of your astronomical observation. Are you ready? Let's go.'

Olivier turned to Xavier and winked at him, before heading off with his mother towards the lift. Xavier went to the doorstep.

'Find a solution!' his son shouted as the sliding lift doors closed.

Xavier didn't sleep that night. The next day he arrived at the agency and didn't say a word until lunchtime. All morning he and Chamois remained silent, the only sound being the clicks of their computer mice.

'I need a woman's advice!' Xavier suddenly announced out loud, throwing down his pen and leaning back in his rolling chair. Chamois looked up at him.

'For… for… for… for an apartment?'

'No, for me,' Xavier replied. 'Your girlfriend, who is waiting for you outside,' he said, jerking his chin at the window. 'Ask her to come in, I need to speak to her.'

'A-A-A…' Chamois sounded fearful. 'A-A-Anne-Laure?'

'Yes,' said Xavier. 'Anne-Laure, if that's her name. Get Anne-Laure to come in, please.'

*

'Good morning, Anne-Laure,' Xavier began. 'Make yourself at home. Would you like a cup of tea? A coffee? A soft drink? I have mineral water and even whisky.'

'I don't know…' she said, confused. 'I'd like a coffee, sir.'

'Call me Xavier. Chamois, make us some coffee, if you please.' Xavier sat back down and looked her in the eye. 'I call Frédéric "Chamois" because I think it's more original, and it makes me think of a chamois, the animal he's named after.'

Anne-Laure turned towards Frédéric, looking a little taken aback. He reassured her with a brief movement of his head which seemed to say: the boss is a bit strange, but he's harmless. She turned back to Xavier while Chamois headed to the coffee machine.

'I need a woman,' Xavier continued. 'A woman's opinion… You're a woman – younger than me, certainly, but you have a female brain, and I want to know how that works.'

'You want to understand women?' she said, with a half-smile.

'I'm not that ambitious. Let's say I want your opinion on something recent and specific.'

'I'm listening, Xavier,' she said, as Chamois placed a coffee in front of her.

'I've been watching a woman from my balcony through a telescope,' Xavier began.

'You're a maniac,' she replied, stirring her coffee with a teaspoon.

Xavier grimaced and shook his head. 'That's the worst part of this whole business,' he said.

'Is there a good part?'

'Yes. I'm not a maniac.'

'Go on…' said Anne-Laure, after a sip of coffee.

'Here goes.'

So, Xavier told her everything, from the beginning; from the telescope he had found to the aperitif at Luigi's house; the apartment viewings; to the secret plan to sell his own to Alice. Chamois listened attentively from his desk, as did Anne-Laure.

'So, in summary,' she concluded. 'You're not a maniac, but you are an idiot.'

'How do I get myself out of this?' Xavier sighed.

'I can only see one solution,' she said, after a moment. 'You need to tell her what you just told me. Write her a letter.'

Xavier closed his eyes. 'If you received a letter like that, would you respond to it?'

She was quiet for a minute. 'I'm not sure. But I'm not sure that I wouldn't reply, either. I'd see that you'd made an effort to be honest and I'd see…'

'What?' asked Xavier.

'Proof of love. A great proof of love,' Anne-Laure said, looking at him. Chamois agreed, nodding his head.

But this great proof hadn't led anywhere. Anne-Laure had been wrong. Xavier turned off the meditation session, gathered his things and left for the agency.

'A-,' Chamois began, rising from his seat at Xavier's arrival. 'A-A-A…' Xavier looked at him patiently, waiting for the sentence beginning with the first letter of the alphabet to materialise. 'A-A-Alice Capitaine… left a letter for you on your desk.'

At that moment, a thunderbolt struck the mast. The Spanish ship the *Astrea*, under the command of Don José de Córdoba, swung left and tipped sideways so far that Guillaume feared it would capsize there and then, in the ocean off the Cape of Good Hope. The streak of flame ran through the rigging and set fire to the outer jib. The men rushed forward with pails of water, but their captain ordered them to cut the sail free with their axes – better to lose it than set the rest of the ship alight. So much for the Cape of Good Hope… Guillaume clutched the mainmast, hugging the wood like a long-lost friend. The ship gave a loud crack and the men all shouted out before gathering on the starboard side, using their combined weight to tip the hull the other way. Guillaume was lifted off the bridge, but still clung tight to the mast. A huge wave was bearing down on the *Astrea*, high as a castle wall. Guillaume watched it, seemingly motionless in its great, watery splendour, were it not for the roar it emitted as it threatened to break right over them, washing away everything in its path. The wave crashed over the boat, and it seemed to Guillaume that the air all around him had turned to liquid, for evermore. He breathed its cold and salt. Then the wave dispersed, and he caught his breath. His clothes were as sodden as if he had spent an hour soaking in a bath, fully dressed. He coughed and spat. The salt burned his eyes. Was it so very hard to journey home to France? It seemed as if all the heathens' gods were in league against him.

A year and nine months had passed since the failed observation of the second transit of Venus. He had had his fill of life aboard the ships, boats and frigates that had transported him across the seas of India. After the sea mist caused him to miss the second transit, in Pondicherry, he had uttered not a word to anyone for two whole weeks. Those days had felt unreal: his body was in India, to be sure – he could pick the country out clearly enough on a map of the world – but his mind had gone to ground, hibernating like a small mammal huddling in its burrow, to emerge in the first fine days of spring after a long and peaceful oblivion. Over the months that followed, he struggled to recover his skills, and what was left of his mission. Which was to say, nothing much. Still, a handful of observations could be made, and notes taken. And so he had awoken from his torpor and observed a comet, clearly visible in the night sky. He wrote a letter to Hortense about the phenomenon, and about the whims of the heavenly body that had refused him twice over. For the first time, he chose not to burn the letter, but slipped it between the pages of the huge volume, provisionally entitled *Journey through the Seas of India*, to which he referred by its abbreviated title, simply *Journey*. Again, he charted the shipping routes from the Isle de Bourbon to India, proposing alternatives in times of monsoon. He began to write a history of the monsoons, then reread the text one morning, tore it up and threw the pieces into the air from the colonnaded terrace of the old governor's palace. That same morning, he cut his hair using a sabre borrowed from one of his guards and tied what was left in a pigtail at the nape of his neck. It was time to go home to France. To sail back to Isle de Bourbon, and from there to find a ship that would take him to the shores of Louis XV's kingdom. He reached Bourbon in March 1770, accompanied by his chests of seashells. He gave himself two months to secure a passage to France. One year later, he had gone nowhere. As if the seas of India, and her deities – those enigmatic, smiling women with their many arms – had cursed him to remain among them, in their native waters, like helpless plankton. It seemed there was something preventing him from going home to

Paris and Coutances. At last, in November 1770, he set sail aboard a frigate, but the ship was caught in a storm, and forced to turn back to Isle de France at a snail's pace, its hold half full of seawater. The chests of seashells were floating about, and it was no small task to get them out before the ship sank forever beneath the blue waves. 'I am plagued by some maleficent force,' he wrote in despair, in a new letter to Hortense. Finally, in March 1771, after several refusals, he was accepted aboard the Spanish ship of Don José de Córdoba, who declared it 'a pleasure to have aboard Guillaume Le Gentil de La Galaisière, envoy of His Majesty the King of France, for a voyage to Cádiz, from where he shall journey overland to his home country'. The captain estimated four months at sea. At last, the king's envoy was on his way home to France, eleven years after setting out on a round trip that should have taken him no more than one and a half years.

*

The ship tipped the other way, and Guillaume grabbed a rope to lash himself to the mast. He turned around on the spot and tied himself as securely as the rope master had attached him to his telescope aboard the *Sylphide*, ten years before. The ship rose on another wave, higher than all the others, then raced down into the trough at the speed of a galloping horse, before hitting the surface of the water, as hard as a drystone wall. This is the end, thought Guillaume. He would be lost at sea on his homeward voyage. The ropes he had wound around his body tightened under the effect of the salt, and his volume of manuscript notes, the *Journey*, which never left him, and which he wore strapped across his stomach, dug into his skin. He stared straight ahead, unable to tell the ocean from the sky. Both were the same grey-green. He was lashed to the mast, he thought, like Homer's Odysseus, when the latter determined to stop himself from diving into the sea and swimming to the sirens.

'We are too heavy, *Monsieur l'Académicien*,' the captain told him, in Spanish-accented French. Guillaume turned to look at Don José. 'We are casting provisions and gunpower overboard. Your chests – I don't mean your cases of astronomical instruments, but the others, the ones with the seashells – they are very heavy, Don Guillaume!' The captain struck a note of manly comradeship. And Guillaume closed his eyes.

'If the lives of your men, and our own, are at stake, Captain, then pray do as you see fit,' he sighed.

The Spaniard bowed his head respectfully. Just a few minutes later, Guillaume saw the men of the *Astrea* struggling to reach the side of the ship as it pitched and rolled. Four men were lugging one of the chests filled with the seashells he had collected over so many years. They heaved it up onto their shoulders like a dead man's casket, just before it slips beneath the waves, to be buried at sea. And that's exactly what they did. Lashed to the mast by his own hand, Guillaume watched the same spectacle eight times over, the men staggering under the weight of the chests, then plunging them overboard. The salt water that filled his eyes gave the scene a dreamlike clarity. The marvellous shells from the seas of India returned to their natural element, in the turbulent waters of the Cape of Good Hope. The chests would open in the water and the shells, large and small, round and flat, would dance in the current before sinking delicately to the bottom of the ocean, there to sleep for evermore. And so, nothing remained of his journey. Not even a collection of seashells for the museum.

Nothing.

Close to exhaustion after his dawn climb, Guillaume walked slowly towards the piles of stones. He reached out to touch one of them and catch his breath. There, at the top of the great mountain chain of the Pyrenees, cairns of dry stones over six feet tall stood sentinel at the border between Spain and France. He closed his eyes, then opened them again to look upon the vast procession of peaks that glittered before him in the pale purple haze. The kingdom of France stretched as far as he could see. Best of all, it was finally in his sights. He took a step forward through the cold grass around the cairn. His knee-high black boots had just passed into France. He took a step back, into Spain. He stepped forward once more and stood firm. The eighth of October 1771. The astronomer took out his pocket watch: it was one minute past nine o'clock in the morning. He was back on French soil after an absence of eleven years, six months and thirteen days.

He felt dazzled and overwhelmed – was it the emotion of his homecoming, or the difficult, taxing climb for which he had risen at four o'clock in the morning, with his three guides? Together they had trodden nameless paths along the crests of the mountains, equipped with long, wrought-iron canes that struck the ground with a dull thud at every step. They had slept in a refuge and shared some dried meat that Guillaume had bought from a shepherd, washed down with two litres of red wine. When the cairns came into sight, Guillaume had sunk to his knees in the grass and slowly made the first gesture that came to him, the sign of the cross, followed by a recital of the Lord's Prayer. His guides did the same, kneeling down in the grass in their turn. In their own language, they recited the prayer that united their two kingdoms in the Roman Catholic faith.

*

Don José de Córdoba's ship the *Astrea* had reached Cádiz unimpeded by any further storms after the one off the Cape of Good Hope. During the voyage, Guillaume, resigned to the loss of his seashells and corals, had recovered his spirits by concentrating on his observations of the wonders of the night sky – the great dark expanse that was his world, his life. He gazed in silence at the constellations – Cepheus, Monoceros the unicorn – and the distant galaxy of Andromeda. He noted that the planet Saturn, with its rings, was clearly visible. His observation of Coma Berenices – the strands of Berenice's hair, floating in the cosmos – brought him especial joy. Don José de Córdoba was intrigued by the name, and asked Guillaume to tell him more. The constellation was named in honour of Queen Berenice II of Egypt, who ruled in the absence of her husband, Ptolemy III, who had left to wage war in Syria in the year 246 BC. The queen built a temple to Aphrodite and begged the goddess to deliver her husband home safe and sound from the battlefield. One evening, she undressed and entered the temple naked, with a sharp, cast-iron dagger in her hand. She knelt before the statue of the goddess, then cut off her long braid of hair and laid it at Aphrodite's feet, as an offering. The next day, the tress had disappeared. Conon of Samos, the court astronomer, offered a most romantic explanation: the queen's sacrifice of her hair had so moved the goddess that she had taken it up into the heavens. The constellation he had identified that very night took the form of long, trailing strands of stars. He gave it a name: Coma Berenices, 'Berenice's Hair'.

'And her husband?' asked the captain. 'Did he come back from the war?'

‘Yes, he came home alive, and unhurt,’ Guillaume replied.

Don José nodded gravely. ‘May we both go through life’s journey with a woman who is prepared to sacrifice her hair for us,’ he said, pensively.

*

Kneeling in the grass, on French soil, with his guides praying close by, images of his journey through Spain flashed across Guillaume’s mind: the French ambassador to Madrid, the Marquis d’Ossun, who had received him in fine style, and introduced him to the Bailiff of Arriaga, who had guided him through his first days in the city and saw to it personally that he obtained a pass to cross the frontier, with the 200 piastres he had left – enough to complete his journey to Paris. He had travelled towards Pamplona, along the crest of the Pyrenees to finally reach Bayonne, before heading straight up north to the capital.

He had journeyed overland by carriage, most often on foot, occasionally on horseback, sometimes even on the back of a donkey, and this was how he had begun his ascent though the mountains, before leaving the animal at a farm and joining his guides. On the fifth day of their climb, on a path beside a deep ravine, one of the porters, laden with cases containing his astronomical instruments, had stumbled and lost his burden. The cases had rolled away down the slope for 300 yards or more, throwing up a great train of dust. The poor man had buried his face in his hands, trembling all over, not daring to look at the astronomer.

Guillaume had walked over to his side and placed a hand on his shoulder: ‘It’s nothing, Alipio,’ he told him, ‘the least of my losses. I would rather see my equipment at the bottom of that ravine than your body. We’ll walk on.’

All that remained was his copper telescope, which he carried on his back in its case, slung on a strap across his right shoulder, like a hunting rifle.

Each evening, Guillaume took a quill, unscrewed his bottles of squid ink and wrote notes by candlelight, in his *Journey*. The landscapes were stunningly beautiful, from lush greenery and lakes to vast, unexpected expanses of bare rock, grey and white, with not a single blade of grass, which made him feel, remarkably, as if he was walking on the surface of the moon.

Guillaume rose to his feet and looked up at the sky. An eagle was circling overhead, spiralling from France into Spain and back again. The guides were standing now, too. They walked on together, on French soil.

Xavier,

Let's talk. Come and have a coffee at the museum, I'll be there all afternoon. You write very well. I don't know how to write like that. I prefer to talk.

Alice

Xavier had read and reread Alice's short note, written with an ink pen on a business card slipped into an envelope. Chamois had looked at it, and before he could begin one of his shaky sentences, Xavier said to him: 'Please thank Anne-Laure for me.'

Chamois nodded and smiled. 'So, good news?' he asked in one go, without the slightest stammer.

'Yes… it's not all sorted, but Alice wants to talk.'

'Did she suggest a date?' Chamois asked.

'She told me to come to the museum one afternoon.'

'You-you-you have to go,' Chamois said firmly. 'Now, this afternoon. I'll take care of the agency.'

Xavier was quiet for a moment, then got up, put his jacket back on and looked intently at his trainee. 'Thank you, Chamois.'

'G-g-g-… good luck,' he replied.

Xavier parked in a nearby street and made his way on foot down Rue Buffon, to find himself before the heavy door that led to the museum workshops. He stared at the bell on the anonymous intercom. Talk, certainly… but perhaps just to say goodbye? Xavier took a deep breath, then pressed the button. A man's voice answered, and he replied in turn: 'My name is Xavier Lemercier. I've come to see Alice Capitaine.'

The voice responded: 'Come in.'

The door opened with a jingle of bells. Xavier found himself in the courtyard with the rusty metal animal structures and lifted his head towards the sun. It was high in the blue sky, but dark clouds were threatening. In the courtyard, a door opened, and Alice came towards him, dressed in her usual white coat. They looked at each other for a long moment.

'Let's go into Noah's Ark,' she said, and Xavier asked himself how many women on the planet could propose a tête-à-tête in 'Noah's Ark'. Just one…

In front of the hangar, Alice placed a hand on the keypad and typed in the numbers. The large double-panelled doors opened with an electronic hiss. The fluorescent lights lit up one by one, flickering as they stabilised. The two of them walked under the gaze of giraffes, bison, buffalo, camels and ostriches towards a space in the middle of the hangar, where a brown leather Chesterfield sofa and two large armchairs were arranged around a low table. It was as though a small piece of a British members' club, where one shares fine whiskies over ice before lighting a cigar, had been transported into the animal ark. Was it a meeting space? An enclave converted into a break room? Xavier didn't ask. He sat on one of the chairs while Alice chose the sofa. Xavier noticed that the animal standing over Alice was a chamois with its ears pricked up, looking at him with a smile. There was a long silence, punctured by some metallic clanks: the sound of the sheet-metal roof heating up and expanding in the summer sun.

'I told you I wanted to talk, but now it seems I can't,' said Alice, staring at a lion.

'Me neither,' Xavier confessed, his eyes searching for some comfort in the gaze of a polar bear.

'Animals don't have these problems,' Alice said. 'Their language is very complex, but they would never find themselves in a situation like this.' She looked at Xavier. 'You wrote me a beautiful letter. No one has ever poured their heart out to me like that. No one has ever told me they loved me in such a way before. But…'

'There's a "but",' Xavier sighed, and lowered his head in resignation. 'I knew it was hopeless. It's just like Guillaume Le Gentil.'

'But,' Alice continued steadily, 'if it's going to work out between us, there's something else we need to do first.'

Xavier lifted his eyes to hers. Alice was decidedly more puzzling than he had thought. 'What's that?' he said eventually.

'Something that won't happen again for more than a hundred years. We have to watch the transit of Venus, with our children.'

'You want to come and see Venus with me?'

'Yes, with you, your son and my daughter.'

Xavier nodded his head, as though taking the time to form the picture in his head; he at Alice's side, with Olivier and Esther. And Venus. And the telescope.

'You're charming, Xavier,' said Alice, 'And you seem lost.'

'I am quite lost, I'll admit it,' Xavier sighed.

'No, I don't mean just at this present moment. It seems you've been lost for a long time. I've been lost for a long time too,' she said, closing her eyes.

'We're lost in a great forest,' Xavier said, after a moment.

'Yes,' Alice said softly.

'And we found each other in that forest,' Xavier continued.

Alice nodded and raised her eyes to him. 'You seem worried,' she said.

'I'm beyond worry,' Xavier said with a smile. 'Alice… I'm in love with you. And I don't know how to say it to you, I don't know if I should move closer to you, I don't know what I should do or say.' He felt short of breath, and his head was spinning as if he were standing at the summit of a very high mountain.

'Close your eyes,' Alice said softly. Xavier closed his eyes.

'Breathe,' she began in a voice that was calmer and more serious than normal. 'You are alive. Everything is fine. You are sitting down. Feel the weight of your body, the weight of your feet and your hands. Take note of the sounds that surround you. Concentrate on your breathing.'

That voice. The voice he had heard from his phone during all those mindful meditation sessions – it was the same one. The woman's voice that had disappeared, the one he had been so happy to discover at the touch of a button, often wondering what its owner might look like.

'Alice,' Xavier murmured, half opening his eyes. 'I know that voice.'

'Shh,' Alice said. 'Close your eyes. You can tell me later. Take a deep breath in,' she said. 'Then breathe out slowly.'

Xavier breathed in and out, feeling his heart rate starting to slow. That was it; that feeling of déjà-vu that he had felt when he met her for the first time and which had never left him. No, Alice was not an old friend from the forgotten summers of his youth, or a woman he had met in a shop long ago and chatted to about some book or CD, only for the passing years to bury this fleeting moment in time and erase it from his memory. No, it wasn't her face or her name. It was her voice that he had known before he met her. But she didn't utter those calm, hypnotic phrases from meditation in her day-to-day life. Until now, he couldn't have been certain that the voice was hers. He had had a funny feeling in his subconscious that Alice Capitaine was no stranger, but didn't have the key to this beautiful mystery. It took Alice reciting the simple phrases in her particular meditation voice, like the unchanging ritual of the mass, to finally understand that she and the voice were one and the same person.

'Breathe,' Alice continued. 'Feel the breath entering you like a wave. Leave all your thoughts aside and concentrate on your breath. Life. At this present moment.'

Xavier concentrated on the present moment which seemed unreal to him, and yet, he had to admit, he hadn't felt this alive in years.

'Take note of the sounds that surround you.' There were a few muffled tapping sounds on the sheet metal, which then got louder; drops of water were falling on the roof of Noah's Ark. The storm had begun.

'Think about water, the source of all life. The water of the river, of the sky, of the seas and the oceans. Your shoulders, your neck, your arms and your legs are relaxed. Visualise your body on a beach of fine sand. The sand is as fine as flour, and the blue of the sea is like a turquoise gemstone. You are okay. Everything is okay. Leave your fears behind. Take your time. You may open your eyes when you want to.'

The rain fell on the roof and its musical sound, like a music score from long ago, calmed him. Xavier opened his eyes and saw Alice's face.

'Alice,' he murmured. 'You're here.'

'I'm here,' she replied.

'Alice, I've been hearing your voice on a meditation app for months.'

She smiled slightly. 'Yes, I did that for a while. It's funny that you heard it.'

'No, Alice, it's not funny. It's strange, almost impossible, and quite confusing.'

'Maybe,' she said, before continuing, more seriously: 'Xavier, I'm not just a voice, or a shadow in the lens of a telescope.'

'No,' Xavier agreed. 'You are not just a voice, or a shadow in the lens of a telescope.'

'Luigi says that your friend, Guillaume Le Gentil, spoke of the whims of the stars, with regard to Venus,' said Alice. 'What if the Goddess of Love is playing with us? Why shouldn't the gods have a sense of humour?'

Xavier nodded wordlessly. 'The goddess played with Guillaume, and she's playing with us. Maybe she plays this way during each of her transits across the sun.' Their silence was punctuated by the sound of the rain on the roof, which was getting louder. 'This rain is almost biblical,' said Xavier. 'I wish I could stay in Noah's Ark with you forever.'

'Xavier, let's agree on something.'

He looked at her questioningly. 'What shall we agree on?'

'Let's agree,' Alice continued, 'that we will kiss once the transit of Venus is over. What do you think?'

Xavier nodded. 'Yes, let's agree to that. That's good, otherwise we won't be able to kiss again for over a century.'

'Exactly,' said Alice, smiling before continuing. 'Our children are emailing each other.'

'I know,' Xavier replied.

'Esther thought I didn't know, but I saw her, and I asked her. She confessed to having set up an email account. I didn't say anything; I'm finding her increasingly calm and confident these days. In short, our kids have decided to watch the eclipse with us.'

'Let's watch the eclipse with them. But it's very early,' Xavier said.

'I know, I saw,' Alice said. 'But that's not the problem.'

'What's the problem?'

'The problem is that they have decided on the location between themselves.'

'And… where is it?' asked Xavier.

'The Eiffel Tower. At the top. The highest point in Paris. They've decided they want to see it from there. But it's impossible. I checked the time of the eclipse on the internet, it's too early in the morning. It won't be open.'

The two of them were silent as they mulled over this childish dream that no adult could make happen; the best they could do was watch from the terrace of Xavier's apartment or the balcony of Alice's.

'Come on, let's go and see the rain,' she said, and the two of them stood up and moved along the hangar towards the door, to watch the sheets of rain falling.

'It's summer rain,' said Alice. 'It won't last.'

Xavier watched the waves of water sweeping the courtyard and the metal animal frames, then took out his phone and looked at Alice. 'Wish me luck,' he said.

'What for?' she asked, surprised.

'We will kiss after the eclipse. But take my hand.'

'Who are you going to call, Venus?'

'Something like that,' Xavier replied, and Alice slipped her slender fingers between his, took his hand and looked at him in bewilderment. Xavier searched his contacts list and then pressed the call button. It rang once, then twice, and on the third ring, someone answered.

'Hello, General Delieue?' Xavier said.

'This is he,' replied the officer's neutral voice.

'Sir, my name is Xavier Lemercier.'

'I know who you are, Monsieur Lemercier. You're the man with the telescope.'

'Sir, you told me that if I ever needed a favour…'

'I know what I said, Monsieur Lemercier. I'm listening.'

The rain beat hard, bouncing off the cobbles. Clouds scudded above the houses. Guillaume climbed down from his carriage and the brim of his black velvet three-cornered hat filled immediately with water. He removed it and tipped it like a teapot, pouring its contents into the gutter. He had found a carriage driver by chance at the toll house at Monceau, and paid him with almost the last few coins left to him after his long journey from Bayonne. The coachman was wrapped in a black woollen cloak and wore a leather hat pulled low over his face. He climbed down and unstrapped the single, lightweight trunk that had accompanied this unusual passenger, with no other luggage besides a rectangular case with leather straps which he had carried across his back and preferred to keep with him inside the coach.

'Where have you come from, sir? You have the look of a man who made a very long journey before we met at the toll house,' he told the astronomer.

'Pondicherry,' Guillaume had answered, proffering a coin.

'Ah… I see, now, that's near Meudon, is it not?'

'A little further,' said Guillaume. He held out his last *louis d'or*. 'Get yourself some soup and a decent glass of wine at an inn.'

'Oh, thank you, sir,' said the coachman, doffing his hat. 'Long life to you, sir, and a loving wife and children. Money, and happiness above all things, that's what matters!' he added, with an innocent smile that revealed several missing teeth. Then the coach set off once again with a crack of the whip and a loud clatter of wheels. It disappeared around the corner of the street, itself half lost in the mire of the storm. Paris. His home address. The big wooden carriage door. Guillaume picked up his telescope case and slipped the straps over his shoulders. He grasped the handle of his trunk, along with a string bag containing a chunk of bread, some cured pork sausage and a bottle of wine for his evening meal. He had bought the supplies at the toll house: traders without a licence for a stall inside Paris's city walls would try their luck there. Often, they'd be checked and held at the offices of the *octroi*, where the king's provosts would allow them to sell their merchandise to travellers entering Paris, after levying a tax of their own – a few bottles of decent wine and a brace of game. Guillaume placed his hand on the huge iron knocker and pushed the heavy door. The cobbled courtyard was unchanged, but the tree that grew in the centre seemed bigger. His footsteps rang out as he walked beneath the arched carriage entrance. He passed the stone well in the corner, the huge pail swinging on its pulley in the wind. He found his key in the pocket of his coat and began to climb the stone staircase with its wrought-iron balustrade, entwined with spiralling scrolls of gilt foliage. Second floor, left-hand door. The La Galaisière family's Paris address for three generations. Guillaume had advanced his brothers' and sisters' share of the inheritance, to secure it for himself. No one came here any more. They all lived on the Cotentin peninsula. He was the only one with any business in Paris. Guillaume turned the key in the lock, conscious that there would be no domestic servants waiting on the other side of the door. Henriette and Gustave, his caretakers, had been elderly when he left for the Indies. They had taken the opportunity to request their final payment and had returned home to Normandy to see out their days.

The hallway was sunk in darkness. Guillaume set down his trunk and his bag of food, and felt his way to the salon, where the fading light of the autumn dusk struggled to pierce the shutters. He hit a bulky object that rang with a deep, musical note, like a bell. He almost fell over. The bathtub. He had quite forgotten: he'd had it made by a master plumber, in fine red copper, but the craftsman had taken longer than expected, and it had been delivered on the day he left. Preoccupied with myriad arrangements for his journey, Guillaume had sent the delivery men to his address and told them to leave it there, in front of the sofa. With the telescope case still slung across his back, he opened the three windows overlooking the street and pushed back the shutters. It was still raining. He fastened the shutters back against the wall and closed the windows, then struggled free of his telescope case, placed it on the floor and began to pull back the sheets with which he had covered each item of furniture. Last of all, he pulled back the sheet covering his harpsichord, placed his fingers over the keys and pressed the opening notes of Bach's *Art of the Fugue*. The last time he had played the piece, a large yellow spider had listened, warily. The harpsichord was badly out of tune, and the air was full of dust. Guillaume sneezed five times in a row. He blew his nose on his only remaining cotton handkerchief, and set about making some light, because the day was fading fast. In a drawer of his astronomer's cabinet – the piece had come to him from his master, Joseph-Nicolas Delisle – he found a metal lighter and his flintstone. From another, larger drawer, he fetched six ecclesiastical wax tapers and fixed them into a candelabra on the mantelpiece. With an assured, precise gesture, he struck the lighter against the stone just above each wick, setting them alight. The repetitive strike of metal on stone, and the rain of sparks, reminded him of Louis de Vauquois, the captain of the *Berryer*, who had lit his pipe and his most unusual tobacco, with its aroma of spices and woodsmoke, in just the same way, while a pirate ship bore down upon them. Guillaume could hear him now, as if he were in the room, hollering for the cannon hatches to be opened, before advising him: 'Monsieur Le Gentil, my most esteemed passenger, I suggest you cover your ears.'

The logs laid across the andirons in the hearth were thoroughly dry. Guillaume repositioned a couple, took some kindling from the copper pot close by, then crumpled a piece of paper and lit a fire from the flame of one of the candles.

In his bedroom, he pulled back the dustsheet covering his bed and pinched his nose so that he would not suffer another attack of sneezing. He plumped his pillows, and thought of the small, multicoloured cushions used by the masseuses in Pondicherry. He turned to the large bureau that was placed barely a yard from the bed. It was covered with astronomical charts and notes taken just a few days before his departure. His compass lay over a map of the heavens. He turned the sheet towards him and read: TRANSIT OF VENUS, 6 JUNE 1761. He stood in silence, then pushed the paper away. His eye fell on the ink bottles, their contents dry. He picked one up and turned it upside down. Tiny particles, like charcoal, fell out onto the starchart. He went back to the salon, fetched the string bag and crossed to the kitchen to cut some slices of bread, and dice the sausage which he would eat from the point of his knife. He took out a delicate, wrought-iron bottle-opener with a so-called Archimedes screw, uncorked his wine and took a long drink straight from the bottle. He finished the bread and sausage, and thought he might take a bath. It was certainly too late to call for a water-carrier. Guillaume opened the cupboard containing his cooking utensils, took out a big, brass cauldron and placed it in front of the fire. It was big enough, and he could hang it from the rack over the hearth. He left the apartment and went downstairs to the well in the corner of the courtyard. He released the bucket, which plummeted a good 100 feet on its chain. Guillaume heaved it back to the surface on the pulley, then lugged the five gallons of spring water back up the staircase, hung the cauldron over the fire, and carefully transferred the contents of the bucket into it. He repeated the operation, from the well to the hearth, six times. Between each return trip, he emptied the boiling water from the cauldron into his bathtub. Almost an hour later, pouring with sweat, he closed the door to his apartment, took a last swig from the bottle of wine and unwrapped the curious 'cake of soap' which his apothecary had procured for him the day before his bathtub was delivered. A cake all the way from the Levant, stamped with a mysterious seal. The marbled green-and-yellow cube was scented with olive oil and laurel.

Guillaume undressed. He took off his silver-buckled shoes, his white stockings, and his frock coat, its rich blue faded by the bright sun of the Indian seas. He removed his shirt and his cotton underpants. He stood naked. All that remained was to unstrap the *Journey*, which he carried around his waist, so that everyone he met thought he had something of a pot belly. Or perhaps, more poetically, he was pregnant like a woman – with a book. An astronomer carrying a marvellous journey in search of two eclipses, neither of which he had seen, nor would ever see. The leather straps that had chafed his skin fell to the floor with a slap that rang out across the room. He placed the 400-page block of notes, sketches, drawings and diagrams on a low table then looked at the steaming bathtub. For a second, he saw again the dolphins breaking the surface of the water, then spiralling up into the air, when he had swum out from the *Sylphide*. Guillaume closed his eyes then climbed carefully into the scalding water.

Half an hour later, he lay stretched out, immersed in warmth. The salon was filled with steam, the embers of the fire glowed red in the hearth, the soap cake had washed him clean, and Guillaume's arms lay – dangled – over the rolled copper top of the tub. He stared at the ceiling and thought to himself that this time, at last, he was truly home. He had bathed in the bluest waters on Earth, seen the most astonishing fish, and almost capsized and died several times. The fabulous seas of India had returned him to his own country at last, safe and sound. He had swum in an infinity of water, vast and blue as the sky, to end his journey here and now, in this copper tub.

'That's enough!' César-François Cassini shouted the words and smacked his desktop, which made the revolving lunar planisphere jump in its stand. 'This quarrelling serves no purpose, gentlemen. The stars are watching, they shall be your judge, and their judgement is far from favourable. Pray leave the room now, all of you, with the exception of Monsieur Le Gentil and His Grace the Duc de La Vrillière.' The Director of the Observatoire de Paris was known for his fits of rage, which could be heard from the far end of the Louvre palace, and which sent perspiration trickling from under his wig in rivulets through the thick white foundation on his forehead. Twenty astronomers rose in the great hall of the Académie and filed towards the doors in order of rank. Their voices rose in animated conversation as soon as they reached the hallway outside. Silence fell in the room, at last.

Cassini stood up and pressed a hand to his cheek.

'Ah, this blasted spot!' In an exasperated gesture, he tore off the black taffeta beauty spot that he wore on his cheek and flicked it across the room. 'It makes me itch. Hideous thing.'

Guillaume remained seated. His wig lay five yards away on the floor. The Duc de La Vrillière sat hunched in his chair, stroking the stump of his left hand, which he'd had to have amputated seven years ago after a hunting accident.

*

It had all begun early that afternoon, when Guillaume had presented himself at the Académie Royale de Sciences in the Louvre palace. He had written to Cassini that very morning, and sent the letter by messenger, announcing his return and requesting an audience.

He wanted to inform the Académie of the forthcoming publication of his *Journey through the Seas of India*, and to share the astronomical observations he had made over the course of his travels. When he entered the foyer of the Académie, the concierge rose to greet him, then stepped forward more and more hesitantly, until he stood rooted to the spot, staring at Guillaume in horror.

'But this cannot be…' he whispered. 'Monsieur Le Gentil, you are dead.'

'I assure you, Octave, I am not dead, or I should not be standing here now.'

'Ah, but no!' the other replied. 'Ghosts exist, I've seen them myself. A great many in this palace alone. I sleep here, I know… Believe me.'

Guillaume smiled and carried on walking towards the great staircase. He wore a satchel over his shoulder containing the day's announcement. Cassini's office was empty, and a lackey indicated that the master was waiting for him in the Etruscan Room – one of the vast lecture halls of the Académie. Guillaume made his way there. The heavy, gilt-encrusted door opened and a loud hubbub of conversation reached him from inside. His confrères were gathered on thirty or so chairs, while Cassini had installed himself at his desk on the podium. Guillaume stepped over the threshold, and the conversation dropped to low murmurs, whispers and coughing. Walking down the aisle to the front row, Guillaume caught the eye of several people he knew. Some stared fixedly at him; others smiled and nodded. He had imagined a less formal, more amicable reception. Sitting in the front row, the Duc de La Vrillière greeted him with warm enthusiasm and held out his right hand. Guillaume saw that His Grace had lost the other while he had been away. He turned to Cassini, who looked vexed behind his desk.

'Master,' Guillaume bowed his head respectfully. 'Thank you for this audience.'

'Veteran academicians never get one so quickly!' called a voice from the back of the room. Guillaume turned to look at the man who had spoken.

'I do not know you, sir,' he said, 'but I am no veteran. I have never given up my Chair. I remain an astronomer of the Académie Royale des Sciences.'

Cassini cleared his throat and fiddled nervously with his wig.

'Monsieur Le Gentil,' he began, 'my very dear confrère, your absence – and what an absence! Twelve years… – has, and I regret very much to say this, changed a great many things. All of us believed you dead.'

Guillaume glanced at the duke, who returned his gaze, nodding pointedly.

'In the fifth year, the question of the reattribution of your Chair was raised, but I postponed it until the seventh year… You have no Chair at the Académie, Monsieur Le Gentil, but you were made a veteran, with all due privileges.' Guillaume remained standing but dropped his satchel to the floor.

'You have retired me,' he said softly. 'You have retired me!' he repeated, much louder, turning to face the rest of the room, which sat in silence. He turned back to Cassini, who swallowed, equally soundlessly.

'We had no news from you,' ventured one astronomer.

'And my letters? I wrote to you at the Académie! I wrote to His Grace the Duke, too.'

'Your letters must have been lost at sea, Guillaume,' said the duke, tentatively. 'You were so far away, and all I received was a single seashell.'

'I have given my life to our pursuit of science. I have crossed oceans…' Guillaume's voice shook.

'And you failed to observe Venus. Twice!' called one of his colleagues.

'There was a sea mist!' Guillaume called back. Scattered laughter rose at his words. 'What do you know of the mist in Pondicherry, sir?' he challenged. 'You, who have never seen a star beyond the confines of the Mediterranean?'

'Gentlemen!' Cassini called the room to order. A long silence followed.

'You were reported missing, or dead, my dear confrère,' said a voice from the floor, in justification. 'We had no choice but to reattribute your Chair.'

'Then I am nothing! Is that it? Nothing! Though I have seen more than your eyes will ever behold, your whole life long. This is intolerable!' Guillaume shouted the words, tore off his wig in fury and threw it to the floor. Voices were raised around the room.

'Take back your wig!' cried Cassini. But Guillaume simply took his seat, folded his arms across his chest and stared out of the windows, into the stream of afternoon sunlight.

Some of them had thought him dead; others had received news but told no one. Still others defended him, but they were in the minority. Rumours of every sort had been rife: that he had become a smuggler in the seas of India; that he had married; that he was living in a monastery in Manila; that he had renounced astronomy, made his fortune, and lived a life of indolent luxury in a palace, surrounded by slaves; that he had changed his religion, or was living modestly as a fisherman in Madagascar; that he had gone mad, or lost his memory, or was settled in China…

The duke tried to speak to the floor: 'In the words of Michelangelo, the sun is the shadow of God: my protégé, your fellow astronomer, became an explorer, an honourable transformation – he has much to teach us about the world, and God's creatures!'

But his voice was lost in the din, until Cassini smacked his hand on his desktop and brought the session to a close.

*

The room was silent. Cassini had broken his skin when he tore off his beauty spot, and a thin trickle of blood ran down his cheek. Guillaume sat in silence.

'The king,' said the Duc de La Vrillière. 'We must ask His Majesty to restore Guillaume to his Chair.'

Cassini nodded.

'Your Grace is quite right. Only the king has the power to do it and do it he will. Guillaume, do you hear? The king will intervene on your behalf. Your Grace, I charge you to solicit His Majesty in this matter without delay. Guillaume, you have doubtless returned from India with a thousand valuable observations. I hope you will make them into a book.'

'I have begun to write it,' said Guillaume quietly.

Cassini understood his astronomer's distress, and the hurt he had suffered, never having anticipated he might be relegated by his own brethren. Men were bad creatures indeed. The master of the Académie rose and stepped down from his podium. He placed his hand on Guillaume's shoulder.

'I'm proud of you, Le Gentil,' he said.

Guillaume looked up into his face. 'Thank you, Master. I am proud to have been His Majesty's Envoy.'

'His Majesty will show his appreciation,' said Cassini.

'Master… You are bleeding from your right cheek.'

Cassini took out a handkerchief, tapped his face and saw that the cotton was specked with blood.

'Ah, that damned spot!' He hurried from the room.

The duke laid his remaining hand on Guillaume's knee. 'I am proud of you, too, and I am eager to read your book.'

'Thank you, Your Grace,' said the astronomer.

'Guillaume, you must go to the Cotentin. And very soon. I fear that your family, too, will be less welcoming than you imagine. They have set everything in motion so that they may inherit your fortune, and your land.'

Guillaume closed his eyes.

'One other thing,' the duke continued. 'I have corresponded with a young lady over all these years, the daughter of friends of your family. She began writing to me when she was just a child, and she has asked for news of you twice a year, every year. Her name is Marie-Michelle Potier.'

'Marie-Michelle,' Guillaume whispered the name. He was profoundly touched. 'Yes, a dear child, who loved the stars.'

'She is a little girl no longer, Guillaume. She's a young woman now.'

It was 4:35 a.m. by Xavier's watch when the army Jeep turned off at the Pont d'Iéna to speed towards the Eiffel Tower, which stood out against the night sky. Xavier, Alice, Esther and Olivier were in the back seat, while two army officers rode in the front. Xavier and Olivier had met Alice and her daughter at their apartment, with just enough time for coffee and two hot chocolates for the children. All of them shared the tired, excitable feeling of waking up early – the feeling of going on holiday, catching a plane from the airport at night to take you to the other end of the world, or getting in a car for hours on the road towards the mountains or the beach. Xavier had placed the telescope on Alice's sofa, having carefully folded it up and placed it in its case with the leather straps.

'We've learned a lot about the Eiffel Tower,' Esther had announced with authority, putting down her bowl of hot chocolate. 'You can ask us questions about it while we're climbing up.'

'Me too,' Olivier chimed in. 'I know how many bolts it has.'

'Shh, not now,' Esther replied.

'And what about Guillaume Le Gentil?' Xavier asked.

'He missed an eclipse of Venus in 1761, and another one in 1769,' Olivier replied. 'Then he came back, and everyone thought he was dead.'

'And?' Esther said, playfully.

'And he got married to…'

'Ah, shh now,' Alice interjected with a knowing smile. 'You can tell us that while we're climbing up the tower.'

Xavier's phone rang; the soldiers were outside the building, right on time. Everyone stood up. When they opened the carriage door, men in army fatigues carrying French Army rifles saluted them and politely asked them to confirm their names, which they did by handing over their ID cards.

'Olivier?' one of the soldiers asked, smiling at the boy, and then turned to Esther, who pre-empted him by saying her name. 'The four of you are here for an astronomical observation from the Eiffel Tower,' said the officer, and they all nodded. 'All right. Let's go,' he concluded cheerfully, before getting in the front seat of the Jeep with the driver. They drove through the streets of the capital, which were dark and almost deserted at this hour. No stars were visible in the black sky. Street lamps lit the storefronts that lined the avenue to the end. The summer air was sweet, and the facades glowed gold in the dark. Xavier and Alice looked at each other as they went through one of the Seine's quayside road tunnels. The orange glow of the intermittent lights flooded their faces, and the speed of the vehicle made them feel as though they were contemplating one another in cinematic slow motion.

The tower became clearer against the sky as the Jeep drew closer. The vehicle passed a bollard and took the esplanade normally forbidden for cars, then parked in front of the southern pillar. A dozen soldiers, some armed, some not, were waiting for them. Alice recognised some Vigipirate anti-terrorism forces among them. Four men were standing on the stone steps. The one on the top step held a piece of paper folded in four in his hand. He was dressed in the beige uniform of the French Army, sported a number of lieutenant colonel braids on his epaulettes, and wore a black-and-gold cap. The three other men wore camouflage fatigues and green berets. Xavier put the telescope on his back, adjusting the straps, and went over to them, accompanied by Alice and the children. The officer gave them a quick nod as they approached.

'Monsieur Lemercier, Madame Capitaine, children – Olivier and Esther – welcome,' he began, in that clipped, military tone of voice customary to his profession. 'On this, the sixth day of June 2012, the Eiffel Tower is open to you, by order of the military commander of the city, the order which I hold in my hand, and which has been signed by the President of the Republic,' he continued. 'This privilege is offered to you in exchange for "services to your country". Sir,' he said, looking Xavier up and down in a cold but respectful manner, 'the French Army is proud of you.'

Xavier gave a quick nod of his head, much to the amazement of Alice and the children.

'The Legion will escort you. Corporals Kamenov, Dos Santos and Plouhinec will climb the tower with you. We cannot activate the lifts, so you have one thousand six hundred and sixty-seven steps to the top. If the children get tired, the corporals will carry them on their backs. The three green berets stood to attention and saluted their superiors. 'Messieurs legionnaires, to your mission!'

'Who *are* you, Xavier?' muttered Alice.

'A man who can open the Eiffel Tower,' he replied with a disbelieving smile. 'Sorry about the steps. There are a lot of them.'

'It doesn't matter,' Alice said. 'Are we on time?'

Xavier checked his watch. 'Yes, I calculated fifty minutes to climb to the top, then ten minutes to set up the telescope towards the east.'

'Let's go, then,' said Alice. 'Let's climb.'

The first legionnaire, Dos Santos, who was easily six feet tall, led the way, while Kamenov and Plouhinec, both considerably shorter and stockier, brought up the rear.

'*Davai, davai!*' Kamenov cried, in what was plainly his native Russian.

'I have water if anyone is thirsty,' said Dos Santos, turning to them on the stairs. 'Particularly the children. If you are thirsty or tired, please say so.'

The metallic steps resonated with their ascent, and they soon gave up counting them. A summer wind that was almost warm rose and blew in their faces as they climbed to the first level.

'So, you're going to see the transit of Venus, right?' Plouhinec asked.

'Yes,' Alice replied, without turning around, as she wouldn't let go of the handrail that allowed her to climb more easily.

'We should be able to see it very clearly from the top,' Xavier added.

'My father is planning to watch it from the headland of Décollé, next to Saint-Malo,' the legionnaire responded. 'Wait until I tell him that I saw it from the Eiffel Tower!'

They reached the first level and stopped for a break and Dos Santos took out small bottles of water from his pocket, passing them to the children and then to Xavier and Alice.

'I think my family can see it from Cape Verde,' he said. 'I sent them a message. What about you, Yuri? Can it be seen where you're from?'

The Russian shook his head. 'I didn't send message,' he said with a strong accent. 'Don't know if you see planet from there.'

'You're from Russia,' said Esther, standing in front of him. 'You come from Putin's country.'

The Russian nodded. 'I come from his country,' he confirmed.

'Your country is huge on the maps of the world,' she said, spreading her hands apart.

'Yes,' said Kamenov proudly. 'My country is the biggest of all countries.'

They continued on up to the second level, admiring the city which shrank with every step they took. The Arc de Triomphe looked the size of a sugar cube, the towers of La Défense resembled a scene in a snow globe and the Dôme des Invalides looked like a golden jewel, discarded among the Haussmannian grey-stone buildings. Esther was out of breath, as was Xavier, who was still carrying the telescope on his back.

'You're out of shape,' said Dos Santos.

'You may have a point,' Xavier admitted.

'Give me your gear,' Dos Santos said. Xavier handed him the case, which the legionnaire put on his shoulders. Olivier too was catching his breath and looking at Alice.

'I think we should carry you,' said Plouhinec to Esther and Olivier. 'Then I can win my bet with Yuri,' he said, winking at his colleague.

'You're going to lose, Breton,' the Russian replied, grinning. 'Miss Esther, climb onto my back,' he said, crouching down before her. Plouhinec did the same with Olivier, and the two children hung on to the soldiers before being lifted as though they weighed no more than a feather.

'Right, let's keep going,' said Dos Santos, and he led the way towards the top.

'*Davai!*' Yuri cried in response. The sky was starting to lighten, turning a purple-speckled blue. Dawn was close; the sun would be up soon. Alice went ahead of Xavier, his eyes fixed on her black boots as she ascended the steps.

'How many bolts are there on the Eiffel Tower?' Olivier asked.

'A lot,' replied the Russian.

'Three hundred thousand,' Dos Santos suggested.

'Five hundred thousand,' Plouhinec guessed.

'A million,' Xavier said.

'Two million,' said Alice.

'Mum is almost right,' Esther announced.

'Two million one hundred thousand,' Xavier tried.

'Two million two hundred thousand,' Alice chimed in.

'Three hundred thousand!' said Xavier. They climbed the steps, betting on the number of bolts until the children shouted:

'Stop! There are two million five hundred thousand bolts on the tower.'

'A lot bolts,' Yuri repeated, satisfied.

'Who did Guillaume Le Gentil marry?' Esther asked.

'Woman he loved, I hope,' Yuri replied.

'Ah no, don't tell us,' said Alice. 'Tell us after the transit of Venus.'

On the third level, at the top of the tower, they opened a gate to reach the final walkway which would allow them a 360-degree view. The vertigo was intense; even birds didn't fly this high over the city. The soldiers put down the children and Dos Santos handed the telescope to Xavier.

'It's all yours, Monsieur Astronomer,' he said with a smile.

Xavier checked his watch. 'Let's set it up towards the east right away.'

Alice took a compass from her pocket and calculated that the sun would rise over the north tower of Notre-Dame. 'Just to the left,' she said.

The round walkway had plenty of telescopes for tourists to use, but those were only suitable for observing key monuments from afar. Xavier knelt down and opened the case to take out the instrument that had accompanied the king's emissary for over ten years in the seas of India; the telescope that had never seen the transit of Venus. He unfolded the iron stand, adjusted the lens, tightened the dials, and opened the three-part brass tube to frame Paris's cathedral in its circular viewfinder. The towers and the spire appeared.

'I downloaded a map of the stars from the internet. I think it should be there, but more to the left,' said Alice, looking through the lens.

'Are you sure?' Xavier asked.

'Yes, it should be right there.'

'I would have said further to the right,' Xavier said.

'I wouldn't,' Alice retorted.

'They're hilarious, they never agree on anything,' Olivier muttered to Esther.

'It's because they're in love,' she whispered back.

The army officers had congregated further away and were putting on eclipse glasses to protect their eyes from the light of the sun, while Plouhinec took out binoculars.

Alice checked her watch. 'It's almost time, Xavier, the sun will be up in thirty-five seconds.'

'The black lens!' Xavier cried, leaping on the box and pulling the black disc out of its chamois leather case, screwing it onto the viewfinder. The city disappeared immediately, and if they were right about the calculation of the angle, the sun would appear in less than twenty seconds.

'To the left! I was right!' cried Alice, pointing towards the east. A luminous dot the size of the white-hot head of a pin had just appeared on the horizon. Xavier pressed his eye to the lens; the dot was growing quickly. Alice was correct: they were at the right angle. The last observation of the transit of Venus for more than a hundred years had begun. The glowing dot projected a ray diagonal to the sky.

'It's now!' said Xavier, emotional, and the whole city was ablaze with light; even the beams of the tower were tinged with orange as if they were molten. The solar disc rose quickly before passing the horizon. Perfectly round, it filled almost the entirety of the telescope's lens.

'It's magnificent,' Xavier murmured. 'Alice,' he said, turning towards her, 'come and see what nobody will see again for more than a century.' Alice put her right eye to the lens to see the solar disc with a clear, precise black marble to the right of it, which seemed to float in front of it as if suspended in oil: Venus.

Alice slipped her hand into Xavier's, who held it in his, then she pulled away from the telescope and they looked at each other for a long moment.

'What about us?' clamoured Esther and Olivier.

'Come here,' Xavier replied. 'I'll crouch in front of the telescope, and you can each take a turn on my shoulders.' Olivier let Esther position herself on his father's shoulders first and she put her eye to the lens.

'I see it!' she shouted excitedly. 'I see Venus! To the right! It's like a big beauty spot on the sun's face.'

Olivier took his turn on Xavier's shoulders and saw the same spectacle of shadows and light in two circles, one large and white, the other small and dark.

They took turns in front of the telescope for the hour that it took for Venus to pass across the sun, and those sixty minutes seemed to pass in a flash. The marble was drawing closer to the edge of the sun when Alice and Xavier realised the children had left them to join the army officers and try on their eclipse glasses.

'The transit is over,' said Xavier. 'Venus is leaving the sun.'

Alice gazed through the telescope, then turned to Xavier.

'The astronomer is avenged,' she said. 'And I just had the most astonishing morning of my life. Our children are happy, and I'm very happy too. Thank you, Xavier. What did we agree on in Noah's Ark?' she asked.

'That once the planet of love had passed, we would kiss,' said Xavier.

The summer wind tousled Alice's hair and Xavier took a step towards her. Their faces were almost touching, and the sweet sensation of vertigo they both felt had nothing to do with their position high above the city. Alice closed her eyes.

'Kiss me,' she whispered.

Xavier leaned towards her until his lips brushed hers. Time had stopped; the city seemed far away, frozen. Its inhabitants, the cars, and the urban noise were nothing but far-off memories. It was just the two of them, beneath the sun, at the end of an eclipse but at the beginning of their love. Their first kiss was like the fulfilment of a centuries-old promise of which they were completely unaware. Only the planet in transit knew that secret. Their kiss grew from gentle to more passionate, and Xavier took Alice in his arms.

'I'm very happy too,' he sighed, and they kissed again.

It was 6:55 a.m. and 7.3 seconds. Venus had left the sun's disc for a century or more.

The horse made swift progress along the country roads of the Cotentin, towards the beaches. Guillaume kept a tight rein and the animal galloped hard through the mist. His welcome in Coutances had been warm indeed – some of the townspeople posted themselves at their windows to see the astronomer, their prodigal countryman, return home from so far away. Some greeted him with a friendly wave, still others went so far as to throw flowers in his path, calling out 'Long live the king's astronomer! *Vive Guillaume*, son of Coutances!' But the same could not be said of his return to the family estate. The Duc de La Vrillière had spoken the truth. Not one of his relatives had made the journey into town to meet him, and in the large, low-ceilinged room, in the last glow of the fire – with a pot of soup still hanging from the rack – silence reigned at their meeting after his twelve years of absence. His brother held him close for several moments, followed by his sister, but their show of affection was as mechanical as the gestures of a pair of wooden puppets, and as cold.

'Mother died while you were away in the Indies,' said his brother.

'I know,' said Guillaume. 'I shall pay my respects at her tomb.'

Three of his cousins sat at the table. They had asked their lawyer to attend, a corpulent fellow with a brick-red face who seemed quite at home, unfazed by this family gathering and the prospect of the icy exchanges that doubtless lay ahead. He had seen other disputes, other successions, and nothing bothered him now. He was the only person present who wore a faint smile.

It was the lawyer who spoke first: 'And how did you find the Indies, sir?'

'Would you like some soup?' his sister asked. 'There's some left. I can rekindle the fire.'

'The Indies are vast, and I won't take any soup,' said Guillaume, sitting down at the table. A long silence ensued, broken only by the soft crackle of the still-burning embers. From somewhere up on the roof, a cat yowled and was answered by a crow, then a dog.

'Do have a piece of veal,' said his brother. He made a show of getting to his feet.

'No, thank you. Why is our family lawyer, Master Tuvache, here in our house, on the day of my return? I doubt you are much interested in my astronomical findings, sir…'

The lawyer smiled, very slightly discomfited now. He reached for a glass of Calvados and swallowed a good mouthful.

'Is that the Potiers' Calvados?' asked Guillaume.

'Yes,' said his sister.

'As good as ever?'

'It's very good,' Tuvache confirmed.

'Indeed,' said Guillaume, 'the Potiers are good and generous souls, they make Calvados from their own apples and offer it to all their friends. Do I have any friends around this table?' The company froze at his question.

'His Majesty's Envoy is here among his own family.'

Guillaume smiled. 'Thank you. I am indeed His Majesty's Envoy, a late returner, but I was entrusted by His Majesty with a mission to journey halfway around the world. My question was not addressed to you, Tuvache, but to my immediate family: do I have any friends among you?' Guillaume repeated his question, fixing his gaze on each of them in turn. He noted that several of his kin looked away.

'What a strange thing to ask,' said his brother. 'Whether you have any friends among the members of your family!'

'It's a legitimate question, in my view,' said Guillaume. 'I made true and loyal friends far off across the ocean. Some are dead, and I hold their affection in my heart.'

He looked towards a chair that had remained unoccupied, in accordance with family tradition, since the death of his grandmother. No one ever sat in it, but the chair was always at the table. Guillaume gave a sad smile.

'Such a shame that she is no longer with us,' he said. 'She was firm, obdurate even, but she was a thoroughly good woman.'

The lawyer frowned and one of Guillaume's cousins leaned across to explain the empty chair and tell him about their matriarch.

'I wish she was here,' Guillaume said, 'to make one of her milky-white kelp soups that smelled of the sea.'

'Guillaume…' his sister said in a low voice.

'Yes, "Guillaume", as you say… Where is Guillaume now? Guillaume the little boy who gazed at the stars, who almost became a priest, Guillaume the astronomer, Guillaume of the seas of India.' He recited the list with a nostalgic smile. 'Well, I've been told you all thought me dead, and that you have begun proceedings to share out my inheritance,' he declared bluntly.

'Yes, we thought you were dead!' His brother spoke up now.

'Everyone believed you were dead. Everyone told us so,' his sister added, and his two female cousins nodded in agreement.

'A man dies when he stops breathing and his body is laid in earth. Who told you I was dead? There were no shipwrecks reported with my name on the passenger list. If anything had happened to me during all these years, there would have been a trail to the proof of my death, but there was none, for the simple reason that I am very much alive.'

'The Duc de La Vrillière told us he had no news of you,' said his brother.

'The duke was never in a position to inform you of my death. Did he say so, in those words?' Guillaume's voice was raised now, but silence was his only answer. A silence broken by the lawyer, after consulting his watch.

'Sir… His Majesty's Envoy… Your land and your inheritance… You have no wife, no direct heir… Everything has been shared out with all due form, between your brother, your sister and their offspring. The succession is legally valid, and to challenge it would be a lengthy process indeed.'

Guillaume stared at them all, then rose and walked across to the sideboard, turning his back. Quietly, he took several deep breaths, then took out the knife forged for him on Isle de France by the master blacksmith, Toussaint's friend.

'I am Guillaume Le Gentil de La Galaisière,' he said slowly, then turned and plunged the knife straight down into the wooden tabletop, making his entire family, and the lawyer, jump in their seats. 'And I have seen,' he added very slowly, seething with rage, 'more skies, more suns, more moons, stars and human beings, and animals on this Earth than you will ever see in twenty generations! I am the king's envoy! The emissary of God himself! And God is my friend. God is with me; he is watching over you all, and he will judge you for what you are. I shall keep my land, and my profession as an astronomer, if I have to ruin myself in the process to pay my lawyers. But I shall do it.'

The family sat frozen around the table. Guillaume picked up his black cloak then left the room, slamming the door behind him. The knife stayed stuck in the wooden tabletop, like a challenge to them all. Everyone made the sign of the cross.

Guillaume strode towards the Potiers' property. His black boots splashed in the puddles left by that afternoon's storm. He climbed the narrow lane to the big farm, surrounded by apple orchards as far as the eye could see. He passed beneath a tree still drenched from the rain. A gust of wind sent a shower of droplets onto his gold-embroidered frock coat. Dark spots speckled the French blue, faded by the Indian sun.

'Guillaume!' cried a man, standing some distance away, among the apple trees. He dropped the wooden pole he was using to beat the fruit to the ground and hurried to greet him.

'My good friend Pierre!' Guillaume was breathless from his climb. 'You are still the keeper of the apple trees!'

'Guillaume!' the other man threw his arms around the faded blue coat, and Guillaume held him tight. Pierre was an employee on the Potier estate, a simple-minded fellow since childhood, but decent, strong, and conversant with the rocks, trees and clouds. Once, at the seminary, Guillaume had written a sermon about him. He had told his congregation that he knew the best of men, a person of such goodness that he would enter the Kingdom of the Lord ahead of everyone else.

'You are back from the stars!' Pierre looked him up and down. 'You're back and you look very fine indeed!'

'My dear Pierre,' Guillaume hugged him once more. 'Are the Potiers at home?' Pierre nodded.

Guillaume pushed the door, and the Potiers greeted him with as much joy as their workman. They fetched their finest Calvados, distilled in 1609, since when it had slumbered deep in their cellar, covered in years of dust – since the time of Henri IV.

'Is Marie-Michelle here?' asked Guillaume. Her father shook his head. 'Has something befallen her? Tell me not – I have suffered so many ills since my return from the high seas. That would be too much to bear.'

'Not at all, Guillaume, she is very well – in the bloom of health. She has gone to visit her Aunt Madeleine, who lives down near the beaches. Her aunt is ill, and Marie-Michelle has gone to spend a week caring for her.'

'Go and see her, Guillaume,' said her mother. 'She will be so happy. She has written to your patron, the duke, all these years.'

'I'll saddle you a horse,' said her father.

The horse climbed to the top of a small rise and Guillaume saw the Potiers' aunt's house below, overlooking the Pointe d'Agon headland. He pulled the reins tight at the gate, then jumped down and stroked the animal's gleaming muzzle while its nostrils flared. He struck three times with the iron doorknocker then pushed the door and stepped into the hallway, beyond which lay a large sitting room with windows overlooking the bay. An aroma of soup floated on the air. He knew this place, having been here several times with the Potiers, long ago, when Marie-Michelle was a little girl to whom he had shown the constellations. A bed was placed to the right of the chimneypiece, and in it he made out the silhouette of an elderly woman. Guillaume approached her.

'Tante Potier,' he said, 'I took the liberty of letting myself in. I am Guillaume Le Gentil de La Galaisière.'

She turned her head to look at him and smiled. 'Guillaume the astronomer! Here you are, back from your voyage.'

'I came back,' he said, kneeling beside her bed.

She placed her bony hand in his and gazed at him, with kindness in her eyes. 'I took a bad fall, and I am very old now. Marie-Michelle, that sweet child, has come to take care of me. Go and see her, Guillaume, she has gone for a walk along the jetty.'

Guillaume's black boots sank into the sand as he climbed the dune, scattered with tufts of grass and dry seaweed carried ashore on the wind. From the top, he saw the long, ramshackle wooden jetty extending out over the Baie d'Agon. Only at high tide was it surrounded by water. Today, the tide was out, leaving a wet expanse of sand and mud that reflected the sky, glowing pink in the gathering dusk. At the far end, on the platform, he saw the figure of a woman dressed in a pale gown, staring out to sea. Guillaume strode down the dune, crossed a shallow pool, and his boots seemed to float on the pink seawater, leaving its surface undisturbed. He climbed the steps to the top of the jetty and began to walk along its length. His footsteps rang out on the wooden deck. The figure in the pale gown turned and shaded her eyes with her hand, to watch as Guillaume's figure approached. The distance between them shrank until they were just a few strides apart. Now the astronomer could see her face. The little, blond-headed girl to whom he had shown the stars was no more; she had become a young woman of twenty, with gentle, regular features and long, chestnut-coloured hair that fell to her breast, pink lips that looked as if they had been drawn with an artist's brush, and large, dark eyes that were turned on him now, and brimming with tears.

'Guillaume,' she whispered, lifting a trembling hand to her mouth. 'Guillaume, you've come back.'

The astronomer stood stock-still, as struck by her show of emotion as she was herself, at the sight of him there before her, alive and well. There was a sudden gust of wind, she swayed, and Guillaume feared the slender young woman, in her billowing dress, would be blown away. He reached out to catch her, then found her clasped in his arms, yielding, her eyes closed. Carefully, he sank to his knees, out of the worst of the wind, holding Marie-Michelle close against him. They remained motionless for a moment, then she recovered herself and half opened her eyes.

'You came back,' she whispered, returning his gaze. 'You're really here.'

Guillaume nodded. 'I really am here.'

'I've been waiting for you for so long,' Marie-Michelle said. 'I counted the days. I wrote twice each year to the duke. I swore I would never marry, until I had proof that you were dead. I prayed every night. And my prayers were answered.'

Now Guillaume closed his eyes. 'One day, a wise man told me that I was not searching for a star, but for love. And that I would find it at my journey's end.'

'Kiss me, Guillaume,' Marie-Michelle whispered, and she closed her eyes. The astronomer drew her closer and brushed his lips against hers. Together, each for the first time in their lives, they exchanged a kiss. Marie-Michelle opened her eyes.

'I brought you two treasures from my long voyage,' Guillaume told her. 'One is from the sky, the other from the sea.' He slipped his hand into his waistcoat pocket. 'A speck of stardust!' And he gave her the tiny meteor that he had collected eleven years earlier, from the deck of the *Berryer*. The young woman took it in her slender fingers, with the same enchanted smile as when she was a little girl. Then Guillaume took out the pearl from the *lambi* and placed it in the palm of her hand. 'I travelled to the other side of the world in search of a black pearl that would cross the sun, and I came back with a pearl as pink as the dawn.'

Marie-Michelle held it delicately between her thumb and forefinger. 'Guillaume...' she whispered. Then she held it up to her eye and placed it over the setting sun. The pearl perfectly covered the sun's disc, and its colour, at that moment, was that of the evening sky.

Epilogue

Guillaume Le Gentil de La Galaisière married Marie-Michelle Potier. They had a daughter, Marie-Adelaïde. Le Gentil spent a number of years completing and editing the account of his epic journey. *Journey through the Seas of India, by Order of the King, at the Moment of the Transit of Venus across the Sun on the 6th of June 1761 & the 3rd of the same month 1769* was published by the royal press in 1779 (the first volume) and 1781 (the second). He continued his astronomical observations for the Académie, lost his court case against his family, and lectured extensively on the Indian Ocean – its fauna and flora, its currents and islands, and the customs of its peoples. He established himself as an acknowledged expert, consulted by explorers planning expeditions to the region.

Guillaume died in the autumn of 1792, at the height of the Terror following the French Revolution, in the apartment granted to him and his family by the Observatoire de Paris.

Nothing is known of his last words, nor indeed his face. No portrait has come down to us – neither a painting, nor a drawing, nor an engraving. Nothing. An internet picture search of his name produces just one unattributed likeness, indistinguishable from that of so many other eminent men of his day. The algorithm cannot admit, it seems, that a famous man could have no face.

But so it is.

Xavier Lemercier and Alice Capitaine still live in Paris. They are still in love. They sold their apartments to buy one together. It is still in the same neighbourhood, and has a large terrace, from which you can see the outline of the Eiffel Tower, and magnificent sunsets over the roofs of the city. Esther and Olivier are now twenty-one years old. Esther recently broke up with the boy she was dating, and Olivier just did the same with a girl he was dating. Olivier is wondering if, in fact, he hasn't always been in love with Esther. Esther, for her part, is wondering the exact same thing about Olivier. For the moment, they haven't spoken of it. Not yet.

Now, Alice is working on stuffing llamas. Meanwhile, Xavier has written a letter to the Observatoire; he would like to donate his telescope to their permanent collection. But in reality, he is not sure he will post this letter.

The next transit of Venus will take place in 2117. In ninety-five years. You, the person reading these lines, will no longer be here. And neither will I. Like Guillaume, we will miss that meeting. But never mind. We are here. Now. I write. You read.

We breathe.

We are alive.

Everything is fine.